THE PROMISE

A PREQUEL NOVELLA

AMY MARONEY

ARTELAN
PRESS

Cover design by Design for Writers.
Map by Tracy Porter.

ISBN: 978-0-9975213-5-1
Published by Artelan Press
Portland, Oregon
https://www.amymaroney.com/

❀ Created with Vellum

For Julie

"Life shrinks or expands in proportion to one's courage."
—Anaïs Nin

PREFACE

The Promise: A Prequel Novella tells the captivating tale of Elena de Arazas, a mountain woman who navigates the terrors of the Renaissance-era Pyrenees with grit and courage.

Elena's adventures create a fiery backdrop for the entire Miramonde Series, which tells the dazzling story of a sixteenth-century female artist and the young scholar on her trail.

If you like gutsy heroines and lush historical detail, you'll enjoy this thrilling, romantic, and beautifully written novella. Don't miss the sneak preview of *The Girl from Oto* (Book I in the Miramonde Series) at the end of this book.

To learn more about the series, visit www.amy-maroney.com.

1

W hite flakes swirled in the air like tiny stars. The beeches and oaks in these woods were still crowned with gold, but snow had sifted through the trees all morning, bringing with it the unmistakable scent of winter.

Scuffing along faint animal tracks that led to the meadow, Elena cast a glance upward and drew her cloak tight around her shoulders. *It's just a warning from the gods*, she told herself. *A flurry and nothing more.*

A swarm of golden leaves took flight from a beech's highest branches, shaken loose by a gust of wind. They cascaded down in long, looping arcs, littering the forest floor with points of yellow light, a silent army of messengers signaling the change of seasons.

Elena plucked a falling leaf as it sailed by and crumpled it in her palm, trying to ignore the throbbing pain in her toes. She had reluctantly jammed her feet into boots at daybreak. Barefoot, she could slip through the world undetected. Not so with boots. As if to prove the point, a dry branch snapped under her heel. In the hushed wintry gloom, it sounded as loud as the crack of a whip.

She halted under an oak on the edge of the meadow, glancing around warily, one hand on her bow.

Then she set off again, irritated at herself. This time of year, brown bears were still foraging in the high country, growing fat on tubers and rodents. And wolves were lolling in their dens, sated from summer hunts. The fact was, no wild thing had ever threatened her in this valley. There was nothing to fear.

She strode across the meadow, eyes aching from the harsh brightness of the snow that drifted over the grass. Mist rose from the hot springs that bubbled near the brook, suffusing the sharp cold air with a familiar softness. The usual frantic activity of songbirds and damselflies was strangely absent. It was as if the shock of snow had sent every living thing into hiding.

Her refuge was close now, hidden in a grove of black pines. Elena's strides lengthened. The exhaustion that had haunted her steps all day vanished, replaced by a heady buzz of anticipation.

And then she saw it. A thin plume of smoke curling up from the roof of the cabin.

Someone was inside.

She stood motionless a moment. Then she moved quickly into the woods, circled around behind the cabin, and slipped into the cover of a crooked pine whose lower branches dipped nearly to the ground. Pulling her dagger from its ragged sheath, she weighed the blade in her palm, listening. The snow had muted the usual forest sounds—the rustle of leaves, the creak of wood. Even the crows that usually rasped in these trees had gone silent.

"Well?" A man's voice rang out. "Are you going to show yourself?"

She stayed quiet, gripping the dagger's handle. Her heart pounded furiously against her ribs.

"I know you're there." He spoke the mountain dialect, but his words were flavored with some foreign tongue. "You're welcome to share this lodging with me."

At that, Elena could not contain herself.

"I'm welcome to share my own cabin with a stranger?" she shouted. "How hospitable."

A tall, rangy man appeared around the corner of the stone walls. He wore a black wool vest over a white blouse. Dark wool leggings spilled over the tops of his boots. His hair was drawn back in the manner of the Ronzal shepherds, but he wore his beard shorter than they did.

"Your cabin?" He took a few steps forward, peering into the woods. "The shepherds of Ronzal told me I was free to use it."

"Did they? Who do you know from Ronzal?"

Elena backed into the shadow of the crooked pine. A crow chose that moment to rouse itself, scolding her from a high branch. She sighed in exasperation, flinging it a murderous glare.

"I know Jorge de Luz. And others." The man moved closer still, his boots crunching the dry snow.

"Who are you, then?"

"Xabi. Xabi the Basque."

The fear in her chest eased. Concealing the dagger behind her skirts, she walked into the light.

"The shepherds and the monks speak of you, Xabi the Basque."

He folded his arms, eyeing her. "What do they say?"

"They say you're a man of honor."

"I'm relieved to hear it. But I'm still waiting for your name."

"Elena."

"Elena...?"

"I've no other name, but if you require one, I suppose you can call me Elena of Arazas."

"Well, Elena of Arazas, no one told me this cabin belongs to you."

He was dark, darker than her, and so lean that his cheekbones jutted out at stark angles. His brown eyes were solemn under thick black brows.

"I built it," she said. "With the help of friends. It's as fine a place as any to spend a winter."

"You winter here?" He looked skeptical.

"Why not? This valley's low enough to be clear of the worst snows, and well hidden away."

"What do you eat?"

"Your food, tonight," she snapped. "As you've made yourself at home."

He raised an eyebrow. "I have a stew on the fire. You're welcome to share it."

She regarded him in stony silence.

"You can sheathe your blade," he said. "I know the rules of hospitality."

The crow screeched once more and vaulted from the tree. They watched it wing away over the meadow, its black feathers stark against the falling snow.

Elena's fatigue welled up again. Her knees felt loose and a dull pain pulsed behind her eyes.

"Fine," she said. "Let's eat."

She followed Xabi to the cabin, the hilt of her dagger hard against her palm.

2

The cabin was tiny, made of stones that Elena had collected over a period of years. Jorge de Luz and other Ronzal villagers had helped her fit the stones together, frame out the doorway, and build a roof. The oak door was trimmed with iron nails and hardware that were gifts from Brother Arros. He often gave her small items in exchange for the herbs, honey, and healing plants she brought to the monastery.

Hanging from an iron chain above the fire was a kettle filled with stew. Elena smelled garlic and meat, mixed with another pungent odor she could not identify. She was suddenly aware that she had not eaten all day.

A dog lay under the wooden bed frame built into one wall, watching her. His golden bulk barely fit in the space. Around his neck was a spiked iron collar.

Xabi pulled the only stool in the room closer to the fire. "Please, sit."

She unclasped her cloak, sheathed her dagger, and sank down on the stool. Xabi busied himself scooping stew into two wooden bowls. He handed her one and squatted down opposite her. She spooned up a tentative bite. The stew had a strange flavor she wasn't sure she liked, but hunger drove her to take another taste. Then a feeling of tingling heat took hold of the inside of her mouth.

"What's in this?" she asked, eyes narrowed.

"Basque cooking is spicy. We like our peppers." He pulled a leather sack off a hook on the wall and uncorked it. "Wine cools the throat."

Elena took the sack and drank deeply.

"Your throat, maybe." She drank again.

He slid another log on the fire and poked the embers with a stick.

"Seems a bit isolated for a winter lodging," he said. "Game must be scarce."

"That's why I come here in autumn. When I'm not hunting, I'm digging for tubers and searching for mushrooms. There's a smokehouse at the other end of the meadow, and a cache made of stone."

He looked at her. "This snow must worry you, then. Your gathering season grows short."

Elena shrugged. "I never worry about the weather," she lied. "What the skies bring is up to the gods. There are other places for me to spend a winter, if it comes to that."

Xabi set down his bowl and stretched his long legs out. Decorative toolwork ran along the seams of his leather boots.

"Those designs," Elena said, pointing at his boots with her spoon. "I've not seen their equal."

"A shepherd must have a few hobbies to pass the time."

"By all accounts, you're a shepherd. But where's your flock?" She peered under the bed again. "Hiding under there with your dog?"

He laughed. "I work by contract."

"Meaning what?"

"I've no sheep of my own. I follow the flocks, find work where I can. Lately I've found work in Jaca come springtime. If I must, I overwinter with a flock in the lowlands, but I prefer to return to the mountains."

"Why do you not go back to Basque country, to your people?"

"My sister inherited the household and the rest of us had to find our own way. I'll go back one day. For now, it's too far to travel there every year."

"You wander, then? Like me."

Xabi shrugged. "I travel to where the work is. I'd not call that wandering."

"I also travel to where the work is," Elena said.

"And what work is that?"

"Healing the ill, helping babies into this world. And hunting everything in the forest that heals. I harvest plants in the spring, bring them to Brother Arros at the monastery. Sometimes I stay for a while and help in his infirmary."

Xabi nodded. "Johan Arros is a good man."

"How long have you known him?" Elena asked.

He stirred the embers again. When his face was in repose his eyebrows formed two slightly uphill lines, like the angles of a low-pitched roof. It made him look sad, she thought.

"A few summers ago I visited San Juan de la Peña and contracted with the monks to take a flock to the high pastures for summer," he said. "Just before I left, a pilgrim on the route of Camino de Santiago came to the monastery with a terrible injury. He'd been attacked by a bear. Face ripped to shreds, skin hanging off like strips of parchment. Brother Arros had seen me sew up the skin of injured sheep. He figured I might as well try sewing up that pilgrim. I used an iron needle and flax thread. The fellow wasn't much to look at, afterward, but he survived."

She took that in, watching the firelight throw shadows on his face. She had heard the story before. Last spring, Brother Arros had described to her the terrible wounds of a pilgrim who incited the wrath of a bear—and the talents of a Basque called Xabi, who wielded his shepherd's tools to stitch up the man's face.

The wariness that had gripped her all evening drained away. In its place came a sudden tug of desire.

Elena stood and unrolled the furs that lay at one end of the bed, spreading them in a single layer over the planks.

"I'll sleep here, on the other side of the fire," Xabi said, watching her steadily.

Elena held his gaze and pulled her long, dark hair loose from its braid. Then, slowly, she unspooled the length of blue wool wrapped around her waist. "Join me if you wish. We might as well find out tonight if we can stand one another. In the morning, we'll decide whether you'll stay or go."

3

AUTUMN, 1483

Clumps of melting snow fell from the branches of the tall pines onto the cabin's roof, jolting Elena awake. Bright sunlight seeped in around the door frame, making a rectangle on the stone floor. Within a few hours the filmy layer of snow that blanketed the meadow would disappear. Yesterday's storm had been only a taste of winter after all, a warning sent from the gods.

Elena slid out from under the weight of Xabi's arm. In silence she dressed, slipped her quiver and bow over her shoulder, and pushed open the door. The dog pressed through behind her. She strode to the meadow, watching as the dog trotted ahead to the brook and drank, the sun glinting off his thick coat. A haze of steam rose from the warm pools along the banks and a pair of damselflies raced low over the water. She smiled when she heard the throaty trill of a snow finch. All was well again—the world was coming back to life.

It was a good day to hunt. Forest creatures would scavenge madly, spurred by the strange snowfall into stuffing their winter caches full of food. She threaded her way through the trees to her own cache, tucked into a northern-facing slope. The snow here had not melted at all. It might even last until winter's grip descended on the landscape for good.

The boulder in front of the cache's low door took a few moments to dislodge. When she finally poked her head inside, she was relieved to see no sign of disturbance from rodents or other animals. The stone walls were solid, the floor a heavy slab of granite.

There was the crunch of footsteps on the snow behind her.

"The dormice haven't discovered this place?" Xabi asked. "Did you cast some magic spell upon it?"

She stood and turned to face him. Wrapped in his heavy wool cloak, he looked like a solidly-built man. But underneath those layers was a body as sinewy as her own.

"The aid of magic would be most welcome, but it's never been of use to me. No, the only way in or out of the cache is through this opening. A mouse, no matter how strong, cannot budge a door hewn of stone."

She began to muscle the boulder back into place. In two steps he was at her side. Together they slid the boulder across the opening.

"Let's hunt," she said. "The first hour after sunrise is a lucky time for me."

"If it's as lucky as the first hour after sundown proved for me last night," Xabi said softly, "we'll have a bear to skin by mid-morning."

A smile lit up Elena's face, and she let her eyes rest on his for a moment. Then she turned and began striding up the steep slope, heading north.

❄

They returned from hunting with two rabbits, which Elena immediately skinned and butchered. Xabi began splitting wood for a fire.

Elena went to the meadow, the dog at her heels. He raced crazy circles on the grass, which bore few traces of the snow that had covered it last night. Laughing at the sight of him, she stripped off her clothes and slid into the steaming waters of a bubbling spring-fed pool. Quickly she rinsed her body of sweat and rabbit blood. From a leather pouch she took a handful of dried lavender steeped in its own oil and rubbed it into her hair. She closed her eyes, breathing in the restorative scent. When she opened them again, Xabi was next to her in the water.

"You smell like summer," he remarked, picking up a strand of her hair. He held it in his palm, where it coiled like a small black salamander against his skin.

She scooped out another handful of the lavender and rubbed it into his scalp. "So do you."

He smiled, closing his eyes as she smoothed back his hair and ran her fingers over the angles of his skull.

"There is not a bit of extra on you," she said. "Nothing to spare. Perhaps you don't get enough to eat. Have you been spending too much time with the monks?"

"Ha. They're the worst cooks I know. I bring my own salt when I eat at a monastery. I offered it to Brother Arros once, but he refused."

"He's accustomed to flavorless food. I, too, have offered him salt. And herbs. But he'll have none of it."

Elena settled under Xabi's arm, watching the steam rise around them. Long golden rays of late afternoon sunlight streamed across the meadow. The dog snapped at damselflies on the other side of the stream.

"I eat plenty," Xabi said. "I've always been like this. Am I not pleasing to you?"

With his fingertips he traced a path from her neck down each knob of her breastbone, around the curve of her ribcage. His hand settled at the very base of her belly, igniting a wild flutter somewhere deep inside her.

"Yes, Xabi." She leaned into his touch, her heartbeat quickening. "I like you as you are."

4

AUTUMN, 1483

The days grew short. Dark clouds scudded across the sky, sometimes opening up to let tawny light fall across the meadow. When that happened, Elena stopped what she was doing and raised her face to the sun. Soon winter's grip would take over the land and heat would be only a memory.

In the evenings, Xabi tooled leather and she sewed rabbit skins into a blanket. She used the curving iron needles that he kept in his shepherd's toolkit, threading them with long lengths of sheep gut that he had trimmed and dried. As they worked, she told him stories of Basajaun and Tartaro, the gods of the mountains. Xabi told her of his family in Basque country, of the people he had met on his travels.

One night as they undressed for bed he traced the ridges of the burn on her arm with his fingertips.

"How'd you get this?" he asked.

She frowned. "It's an ugly scar with an uglier story behind it."

"When did it happen?"

"When I was a child."

"Was it an accident?" His voice was gentle.

"Some would say yes."

"But you think otherwise?"

"Xabi!" she said in exasperation. "Stop asking me questions. Tell me a story."

He sighed and tucked the furs around them.

"When I first left home in search of a livelihood," he began, "I went west to stay with a cousin on the seashore. The villagers spent their days fishing. They gave me the job of patrolling the beach in search of treasures. I never grew tired of poking at the strange things that washed up—long ropes of glittering seaweed, red crabs, broken birds, fish with their eyes missing and half their scales sheared off."

Elena relaxed, listening to Xabi describe feathery drifts of seafoam on the pale sand, the raucous shrieks of gulls, the slick bodies of dolphins leaping from the water. He told her about the seals that bobbed just offshore, moving silently through the churning waves and surfacing near the beach, their dark round eyes fixed on him.

"Did you see monsters?" she asked dreamily. "Brother Arros used to tell me stories of the sea when I was a child. He spoke of monsters with fearsome teeth and snapping jaws."

"When did he go to the sea?"

"As a young man. He walked to Compostela along the pilgrim's trail."

"I suppose some might call a whale a monster, though the one I found had no teeth."

Elena sat up, her eyes alight. "You saw a whale?"

He nodded. "After a fortnight or so, I found a whale that washed up dead on the shore after a storm. The flesh was too rotted to eat, but that was not the true value of the beast.

We wrapped our faces in scarves to ward off the stench and hacked off great slabs of blubber. Upwind, the women piled stacks of driftwood around their iron kettles. All day they tended the fires, rendering the blubber into oil. Then we sold the oil to merchants who used it to fuel iron lamps. I got a bag of silver coins for my part in it all."

"What did you do with it?"

"I bought what I needed to hire myself out as a shepherd, and then I turned east again."

Elena pulled Xabi's face to hers, luxuriating in the heat that radiated from his lean body. He explored her most tender places, finding spots she had not even known to be sensitive. His brown, work-worn hands moved gently on her skin, sending currents of desire rushing down her spine. With each wave of pleasure her tension evaporated until she felt her mind go soft and indolent. Curled under the furs with him, she forgot the dread that had knitted itself into her bones, the anger that carried her through the world. The jumble of dark worries that haunted her simply vanished.

After he fell asleep, one hand draped over her hip, she lay awake for a long time watching the embers of the fire go cold one by one. She had wandered alone through the world since she was a girl, had not shared a home with a companion since her mother's death so many years ago. There were moments of lust, other shepherds who caught her eye. But none of them warranted more than a night in a cabin, or an afternoon in a meadow.

Until now.

Perhaps the gods were smiling upon her after all.

5

On a gray midwinter morning, Elena awoke with a bitter metallic taste in her mouth. Her tongue felt thick and mossy. She thrust her feet into boots, shrugged a cloak around her shoulders and pushed the door open. The pine trees behind the cabin sagged under the weight of the snow on their branches. A short distance from the cabin, she squatted to relieve herself and was overcome by a wave of nausea. Retching uncontrollably, she toppled forward face first into her own vomit.

"Elena?" Xabi's voice was laced with concern.

She rolled away from the mess, her cheek pressed into the wet snow. Curled on her side, she stared dully into the pines, unable to move. It was as if some unseen weight pinned her to the earth.

Then Xabi's hand appeared in her line of sight.

"Come."

She put a hand in his and he hauled her up. Inside, she sat on the bed and watched him remove her boots and slip off her cloak.

"Lie down," he ordered. "You are not well."

She did as he told her. He went to the fire and began poking the coals with a stick, searching for a live ember.

"A life grows in me," she said to his back.

He dropped the stick and turned to her. "Are you sure?"

"As sure as any woman can be."

Xabi stared at her soberly. Then he sat next to her on the bed.

"We can take the child to the Abbey of Belarac, over the mountains in Béarn," he said.

"No." She kept her eyes trained on his hands.

"Why not? It's where children go who have no other place to live. Brother Arros told me."

"He sent me there when I was a girl." She took in a long breath. "The place was nothing but a crumbling ruin. They put me to work in the kitchens. Would you truly want a child of yours to toil as a kitchen waif?"

"Maybe it was like that then, but no longer. Brother Arros speaks highly of Belarac. He says the new abbess is an intelligent woman."

Elena looked at him, astonished. "He's said nothing of this to me."

"Do you know him to be untruthful?"

"Never."

"Perhaps he doesn't want to upset you. It's obvious the place displeases you."

She scowled. "Even if what you say is true, it comes at a price. For a child to be anything more than a servant at an abbey, one must pay with silver, and plenty of it."

"But I can pay," Xabi said. "Our child wouldn't be a servant."

"It's no use talking about this. There won't be a child, Xabi. What's inside me is only a quickening, a pulsing in my belly."

Xabi sighed and put a hand to her cheek. "You can't stop a baby from coming," he said softly.

"I can."

He sat silent for a while, then reached out and put a hand on her abdomen. She batted it away.

"We are both wild things, Xabi. We move with the seasons, chasing the grass as it grows, melting into the shadows at the approach of a bear. That's no life for a baby."

His expression tightened, but he said nothing. After a moment he got up and went outside with the dog.

6

E lena's mother Maria had taught her how to end a life in the womb. She knew which combination of herbs to use, steeped in a bitter tea that was mixed with honey to make it go down easier. The trick lay in knowing how much of the stuff to administer. Too little, and the woman's belly would continue to swell. But too much could be catastrophic. Elena had once watched a woman bleed to death after ingesting a double dose, despite her warnings.

And now, on the first night of a storm that wrapped the cabin in a haze of billowing snow, she would mix up a cup of the brew for herself. She silently recited the recipe as she measured out herbal powders and covered them with boiling water. Then she forced down sips of the mixture, her face twisting with disgust. It tasted like poison.

Xabi tended the fire and watched over her, his eyes creased with worry. When the pains began, he settled her gently on the bed and covered her with his cloak.

By dawn she had a raging fever. Following her instructions, he boiled boxwood leaves and fed her the broth. It seemed to quell the burning of her brow somewhat. When blood began to flow between her legs, he wiped her clean with a damp flax cloth. He pressed the water pouch to her cracked lips and made sure she swallowed, smoothing the sweat-soaked hair away from her forehead.

The moan of the wind forcing its way through chinks in the stone walls did not cease for two more days and nights.

Finally they awoke one morning to silence, and Xabi flung open the door to let in sunshine. They heard the trickle of water released from the long icicles that hung from the eaves. Then came the tentative warble of a song-bird and the whoosh and thump of snow sliding off the pine branches and landing in the drifts below.

"I'm so thirsty," Elena whispered.

Xabi went outside and broke off an icicle that hung from the eaves. He brought it to her. The open door let in the scent of pine.

The tip of the icicle melted against her tongue.

"I feel the breeze," she said weakly. "It's a spring breeze, Xabi."

He nodded, his anxious eyes scouring her face. "Winter's end is near."

The dog bounded outside and foundered in the soft snow. A knot of ice slipped from a pine tree and landed on his head. He snapped at the air, swiveling his neck to get a view of the invisible attacker. Xabi and Elena both began to laugh.

She held her tender abdomen with both hands, willing the hurt to go away, the pain to stop, the quickening to be over, once and for all.

Tears gathered at the corners of her eyes and she blinked them back before Xabi could see. This was the only way. There was no place for a child in her life.

But instead of relief, she felt only sorrow.

7

SPRING, 1484

When the snows had melted enough for them to travel, Xabi sharpened his tools and readied his supplies. It was time for him to follow the shearing cycle through the mountain lowlands. He would begin at San Juan de la Peña, since that was where Elena was headed. When there was no more shearing to be done, he would journey to Jaca, hire himself out, and take a flock to summer pastures.

For her part, Elena would stay a time with Brother Arros, restocking his supplies of medicinal herbs and honey. Then she would make her way to high country for the summer meeting of the mountain people.

The day before they left the valley, they emptied the cache and carried what was left of their smoked trout and rabbit to a high meadow. They left it in neat rows on a flat-topped limestone rock, as an offering to Basajaun and Tartaro, gods of the mountains.

"If a priest spied us doing this, there'd be trouble," Xabi said.

"What priest would climb that high?" Elena scoffed.

"I have heard of them searching for offerings. The shepherds talk of it."

"The shepherds grumble because they leave out cheese for the gods that they'd rather eat themselves. If it's gone the next day they must find someone to blame for it."

"Are you saying they eat their own offerings, on the sly?" A rumble of laughter rose in Xabi's chest.

Elena threw her head back and laughed too. She caught sight of a great bird tracing circles in the sky.

"Griffon vulture," she said, pointing up.

"No." He shaded his eyes with a hand. "Golden eagle."

"Say what you like. I know what I saw."

Crossing the meadow, they spied a slim stone jutting from the ground. It was deeply grooved with carvings.

Elena crouched and ran her fingers down one side of the stone. "It used to be that the mountain folk did nothing but fight. But the peace agreements, the *fueros*, changed that."

"That's what the shepherds in the summer pastures say. Stones like this one tell the people where they can graze their animals, and when." Xabi squatted, examining the marks. "Just how carvings in stone can keep the peace is hard to fathom. I'm not sure I believe it."

"There'll always be disputes. That's what the summer meeting is for," Elena explained. "To work out arguments."

He rocked back on his heels, squinting up at her. "How?"

"If anyone damages a pasture or steals animals, they've got to pay for it with cheese, meat, wool, wood. The people who've been harmed decide what the amends will be."

"The nobles don't intervene?"

She shook her head. "They let the mountain people govern themselves."

"I reckon they're too lazy to climb up here and get involved in the business of shepherds."

"Thank the sun and stars for that." Elena straightened up, frowning. "I've seen what nobles do to the people who live within their grasp. They bring nothing but sorrow and trouble."

She squinted up at a limestone cliff that loomed over the meadow. Approaching it, she drew her dagger from its sheath and began to hack at something.

"What have you got there?" Xabi stood off to the side, watching her.

"Butterwort. Brother Arros needs it for his infirmary." She stuffed the long, hairy leaves into her satchel.

"What else does he need?"

"Boxwood. For fever. Willow, for pain. And star aster, for stomach ache, sneezing, coughing. There are so many more, I can't name them all. He writes my healing recipes in a book he calls his '*Herbal*.'"

"You don't keep hidden any secrets for yourself?" he teased.

"Why should I?" She stopped what she was doing and turned to him. "If I can help him save a life, I will. I owe him every secret these mountains share with me. Anyway, they're none of them *my* secrets, Xabi. They belong to the mountain people, and always have."

When she finished harvesting, they angled through the meadow down toward the woods, luxuriating in the sun's warmth on their faces. Elena spied a darker place in the grasses, a scar in the earth made by a bear's long claws. Clods of soil that it had flung aside now sprouted tiny shoots of grass. She wondered where the bear had sheltered during the months of ice and snow. Perhaps under the tangled roots of an oak tree, or in the hollow trunk of a fire-scorched pine. Now, with the advent of spring, the bear was free again to roam where it pleased.

Like her.

8

SPRING, 1484

A strong late-afternoon wind gusted when Elena and Xabi came to the steep trail known as the Bonecrusher. More than one traveler had been smashed to death by rocks falling from the great white cliffs that soared above it. Despite that, the Bonecrusher was heavily used by smugglers because it was the fastest alternative to the toll road that connected Aragón to Béarn, and wide enough to accommodate mules.

Before Xabi and Elena stepped out to cross the trail and continue along the animal track they followed, they rested in the shadows a moment. The wind died, revealing the sound of voices. They crept through the trees and spied a pair of men standing on the trail, dressed in the black hats and long cloaks that marked them as pilgrims.

"This cannot be the way," said the taller of the two men, his voice tight with anxiety. "Darkness comes and there is no safe place to sleep ahead. It is all cliffs and boulders."

There was a rumble and a clatter of stone. "Saints protect us!" shrieked the smaller man. "A stone the size of my head just tumbled from the sky."

"It's nearly time to make camp anyway," Elena said in a low voice, watching the men with trepidation. "We should help them."

"Pilgrims," Xabi said, shaking his head. "How any of them survive these mountains is a mystery."

Reluctantly they made their way forward.

While Elena built a fire, Xabi went to the edge of a nearby creek and busied himself skinning and butchering the rabbits they had captured that day.

The pilgrims chattered about their journey from a place in the north called Flanders all the way south to Compostela. Their eyes gleamed as they described the holy relics they had seen in the cathedral at Compostela, their fingers endlessly tracing the grooves in the sea shells they wore around their necks. They had been sidetracked on their return journey by talk of a healing grotto in a limestone cavern. Eager to experience the restorative powers of its warm, bubbling springs, they had left the relative safety of the King's Road and blundered into the Bonecrusher.

Elena eyed them as she blew on a smoldering bit of dried moss, teasing it into flame. Perhaps, long ago, when the pilgrims first adopted the habit of wearing identical hats and cloaks it had been a good idea. Now their distinctive garb had become a horn-blast to bandits—though since pilgrims rarely carried anything of value, they made sorry pickings.

"Do you know the cavern of which we speak?" asked the taller man.

Elena shrugged. "These mountains are filled with caves

and healing waters. They're also crawling with wolves and bears."

The men exchanged a worried glance.

"How will we find our way back to the King's Road?" asked the smaller man. His hands clutched the shell around his neck so tightly that his knuckles shone white.

"We'll take you there tomorrow, to the toll crossing."

"What a blessed kindness," the taller man said, relief etched on his face. "God is watching. He sees how good you are to us."

Elena kept her eyes on the fire and said nothing. Xabi returned just as darkness descended, his footsteps silent on the soft forest floor. The dog settled nearby, his watchful eyes on the pilgrims.

When the rabbits were roasted, the pilgrims greedily sucked the flesh off the bones. They protested when Xabi threw chunks of meat to the dog.

His eyes narrowed. "By morning you will likely owe your lives to this dog."

In the silence that followed, the high, wavering sound of a wolf's howl drifted down through the treetops. It was answered by more wolfsong. The dog lifted his head and growled.

"We shall be torn to pieces in our sleep by wolves tonight," the slighter man moaned.

His companion's eyes grew round with terror.

Xabi threw more wood on the fire. "Not as long as this fire burns. Though I'd take care to sleep near the flames if I were you. For safety's sake."

Both pilgrims scrambled closer to the fire and pressed their shoulders together.

"And pray for us," Elena couldn't help adding. "That should help ward off the creatures of the night."

Xabi fought to keep a sober expression on his face.

"Yes," said the tall man, smoothing rabbit drippings into his beard with trembling fingers. "I shall pray for our safety all night. I shan't sleep a wink."

His companion, eyes shut tight, lips moving silently, was already lost in prayer.

9

SPRING, 1484

Elena and Xabi watched the black-clad pilgrims trudge up the King's Road toward the tariff collectors' gates. All morning they had led the men along animal tracks through the forest, climbing slopes so steep that the pilgrims moaned and protested. The two of them, pink faces beading with sweat, had proved as irritating as a pair of buzzing flies. But now, finally, they had said their goodbyes. A breeze funneling down from the white peaks in the north cooled Elena's face as the noise of the pilgrims' complaints faded away.

"Let's take shelter under that pine and watch until they pass through the gates." She pointed into the woods at a tall pine surrounded by dense shrubs. Xabi nodded.

Settled in the shade, they looked on as the pilgrims took their place at the back of a long queue of travelers leading heavily loaded mules and oxcarts.

"They'll have a good rest now, whether they want it or not," said Xabi, taking out his leather water pouch. He offered it to Elena. "I've not seen so many beasts and men in one spot since the wool market at Jaca."

"The snows have only just cleared. This is the beginning of the spring rush."

Elena's mind flickered to long-buried memories of the first time she saw this place. She remembered her small hands clutching the pommel of a saddle, the sound of hooves striking the rocky ground, the sight of Brother Arros's rotund form astride the mule ahead of her. The day when she left Aragón and everything she knew, bound for a new life in Béarn. But Béarn hadn't wanted her—it spat her back over the mountains again, to begin her life of wandering.

Her memories were interrupted by a commotion on the road. The long line of travelers, animals, and carts began to split, peeling from the center of the road to its margins, making way for a group heading south. The crack of whips, the clatter of wooden wheels, the snorting and stamping of animals filled the air. An entourage of knights surrounding an oxcart draped in dark cloth approached.

Xabi and Elena watched in silence from the shadow of the pine tree, hidden from view. When the procession drew abreast of them, revealing the banners draped on the horses' flanks, Elena drew in a sharp breath.

She dropped the water pouch. Liquid pulsed out of it, wetting the pine needles underfoot.

"Which house is that?" Xabi said, his voice low.

"The barons of Oto," she whispered.

Elena stared at the man who rode just ahead of the oxcart. His black horse was the largest in the group, its tail and mane arranged in elaborate braids. The man wore red leather armor and his head was concealed by a polished metal helmet. A great sword hung from his waist.

She clasped her trembling hands together. Without another word, Xabi slipped an arm around her shoulders and she leaned into him. They sat like that until the group disappeared on the road south and the travelers had reformed a ragged line, awaiting their turns with the gate-keepers and the tariff collectors. Taking comfort from Xabi's warm body next to hers, Elena tried to push away the image of the black horse and its rider.

But there was no use. Like the dark fragment of a nightmare, the helmeted man in his red armor had burrowed into her mind.

10

SPRING, 1484

Elena and Xabi slipped quietly south through the forest toward San Juan de La Peña, the dog padding behind them. The dense canopy of branches overhead allowed little sunshine into the woods. They had to reroute often to avoid fallen trees, brambles, and slopes of loose shale. It was by no means the fastest or most pleasant way to the monastery. But it was foolish to travel the main road where any wild thing or bandit hiding in the woods would have a clear advantage in an attack.

And they were in no rush, Elena thought, watching Xabi stride along the trail ahead of her. She heard the gentle clink of his tools inside the leather satchel slung over his shoulders. For a moment, she allowed herself to indulge in a memory of their first night together in the cabin, when she had invited him into her bed and was shocked to discover she never wanted him to leave.

Xabi turned, offering her the water pouch. "Why did the sight of those men frighten you?"

He had said nothing of the encounter until now. Perhaps he had been waiting for some explanation from her.

She refused a drink, stared at him tight-lipped, not wanting to let the helmeted rider back in her thoughts. "The barons of Oto are a cruel lot. Only a fool wouldn't be frightened by them."

"Have they harmed you?"

Elena cast her eyes off to the side of him, watching the dog's tail twitch as it pressed through a thicket of shrubs.

Her fingers formed a circle around her scarred wrist. It was all so long ago. She had spent a lifetime hammering the memories into dust. Why dredge them up again now?

Before she could answer, the warning trill of a snow finch rang out. The dog growled low in his throat.

Xabi's expression tightened. "We're close to the road," he said. "Stay here."

He crept through the underbrush, drawing abreast of the dog. Elena stood with her hands on her hips a moment, then closed the gap between them with a few long strides. Xabi glanced back over his shoulder, throwing her a dark look.

"You should know by now," Elena said, shrugging. "I'm not a very good listener."

The unmistakable moan of a man floated through the trees. The King's Road was visible now. They waited in the shadows a moment, listening for other voices. But all they heard was another feeble moan. They moved forward again. Both of them spotted the man at the same time—he lay in a ditch just off the road.

There was no one else in sight.

They clambered down into the ditch. The man was slight, dressed in the rough homespun of a peasant, his feet bare. No blood leaked from his body as far as they could tell. Upon closer examination, Elena decided his main affliction was an enormous, purpling lump over one eye.

"We're nearly to the turnoff for the monastery," Xabi said. "Lucky for him and me, there's not much to the fellow."

Hauling him up, Xabi draped the man over his shoulders like a sack of wool and began walking south along the road. Weighed down by Xabi's things in addition to her own, Elena felt fatigue set in long before they reached the turnoff. If it weren't for the occasional moan from the injured man, she might have fallen asleep on her feet.

Finally the soaring cliffs of San Juan de la Peña rose up before them. From this vantage point, the monastery was completely hidden behind trees, its dun-colored structures tucked into caves at the base of the cliffs. A small valley lay adjacent to the monastery, and Elena saw the figures of brown-clad monks moving about its fields. Some of the brothers walked behind mules hitched to plows, etching careful rows in the soil. Others cast seeds into the furrows from baskets strapped to their chests.

At the sight of the travelers, two monks stopped their work and offered their assistance. Within moments, the monks had the injured man in their arms and were hurrying ahead to the infirmary.

Xabi and Elena shuffled along behind them, completely spent.

It turned out every room in the monastery's guesthouse was occupied by traders and merchants heading north. Elena and Xabi spent an uncomfortable night bedded down on a nest of canvas wool sacks in the shearing room by the stream.

The next morning, they ventured to the crowded guesthouse, where they found space on a bench at the breakfast table. As the lodgers consumed an unappetizing breakfast of unsalted porridge, stale bread, and weak ale, Brother Arros made steady progress around the table greeting people in various languages.

He had thickened around the middle since Elena was a girl. His monk's fringe had disappeared altogether, and his scalp was pink from long afternoons in the orchards and fields. She had always loved his eyes, which were the grey-blue of the silty waters that flowed from the mountaintops into this narrow valley. When he smiled the lines around his eyes deepened and his whole face glowed with joy. Watching him, Elena was struck as usual by his gift for human connection. Even the most suspicious, reticent travelers warmed to him as if he radiated sunlight.

"This bread is too hard," complained an old man whose black velvet cap, fine wool vest, and tall oiled boots marked him as a person of importance. "I should have had my servants bring some along."

"Oh dear," Brother Arros said. "We've no other bread, I'm afraid."

"We did bring bread, Grandfather," said his companion, a young man with a gentle voice. "Flora gave us a sack filled with your favorite soft white buns when we left Zaragoza. But we already ate them all, remember?"

"Now, Carlo, this is no time for jests. Your wife is a fine woman, but she cares not for the suffering of my belly. All she wants is for you to sell more wool so she can get another rope of pearls fat as chickpeas." The old man's attention drifted a moment. Then he turned to Brother Arros, indignant. "If I had eaten bread on this journey, I would have remembered!"

Brother Arros patted the man's arm and made soothing noises.

The younger man looked down at his bowl and sighed.

"As soon as we arrive in Nay," the old man went on, "send out for bread. Plump loaves of the finest flour, not the coarse stuff that makes my teeth crumble like limestone."

"As you wish, Grandfather."

Elena caught the younger man's eye. He smiled. His face was round, his brown eyes fringed with long black lashes. Poor fellow. Saddled with a grandfather whose mind was turning to mush. The thought of watching a loved one's long, slow slide into madness made her shudder. It was the only comfort she took from her mother's death. At least she would never bear that sorrow.

When the other travelers had finished their meal and filed out of the room, Brother Arros sank down on the bench across from Elena and Xabi.

"The saints above," he said, beaming. "It's always a rare delight to host one or the other of you. But both at the same time! It warms my heart. How did you manage to come upon that unfortunate traveler at exactly the same moment?"

Xabi flicked a glance at Elena. There was a trace of amusement in his eyes.

"It was no accident," she said flatly. "We were journeying together."

"Together? But this is a story that merits telling," Brother Arros said, eyes wide.

"It's a story for another time. First, take us to the infirmary. I want to see that man."

"Very well." Brother Arros made no effort to mask his disappointment. "As usual, I'm to be left in the dark." He pushed himself up from the table and gestured to them to follow him. "Elena's doings are shrouded in mystery," he said to Xabi with a confidential air. "I consider myself very fortunate to hear even the scantest details about her life, though I've known her since she was a tiny girl. I try to chisel away at her secrets, get even the roughest sketch of her adventures. For no one loves a good story as much as I."

"I've told you plenty of good stories," Elena scoffed. "My throat grows sore each year when I come here, from all the talking I do."

"Would that were true," Brother Arros said mournfully. "I shall have to make do with the comfort of your presence, and hope that one day you'll prove more loquacious."

"If I understood the meaning of that word, I might be able to grant your wish," she retorted.

"It means talkative, my dear."

"You should've just said *that*, then."

Behind them, Xabi chuckled.

"You two are like oil and water," he observed.

"Oil and vinegar is closer to the truth," Brother Arros said.

Despite herself, Elena smiled.

11

SPRING, 1484

The infirmary was crammed with pilgrims. Their black cloaks and hats hung from pegs on the walls next to the straw pallets where they lay.

"It's a wonder to me that some of them still walk this earth," Brother Arros said quietly as they threaded their way through the crowded room to the injured man. "They get into all manner of scrapes. Each season brings its terrors. There's the odd encounter with wolves or bears. Those don't often end well. Lately, bandits on the King's Road are the main problem. The demand from the north for wool, wine, oil, and saffron grows with each passing year, and so do the oxcarts and mule trains full of goods. Traders are growing wise to bandits, hiring guards for the crossing. But pilgrims are easy pickings."

He crouched down at the side of the injured man. "Can you speak?" he asked in the common dialect.

The man stared blearily at him from his good eye. The other was swollen shut and circled with blue-black bruises.

"I can," he said.

"These folks took pity on you and carried you here,"

Brother Arros said, jerking his head toward Xabi and Elena. "You'd be dead if it weren't for them, by the grace of God."

"What happened?" Xabi asked the man.

"I didn't get out of their way fast enough."

"Whose way?"

"My mule's ankle grows lame," the man explained. "Sometimes she refuses to budge. I tried to get her out of the road when I saw those nobles coming, but they pounded down at us without pause. I pushed at her with all my strength. Then a big fellow on a horse, dressed in red leather, rode up to me so close I could smell the oil on his boots. He said nothing, just raised his sword."

The man's voice trailed off.

"And?" Elena asked, impatient for the story to end.

"And that's all. I don't remember any more."

"He clearly didn't run you through with his sword," Xabi said. "Hit you with the butt of it, more likely."

"What about my mule? Did he steal her, do you suppose?"

"I doubt a nobleman would steal a lame mule. More likely she wandered into the woods. She won't survive long if that's the case."

The man's lips trembled. "That mule's all I have."

"You may yet find her again," Brother Arros said. "In the meantime, you're fortunate to be alive."

The man looked at Xabi and Elena. "There's not many who'd help one such as me."

Xabi shrugged. "I'd hope someone would do the same for us. Did you get a look at the banners they flew?"

The man nodded.

"What did they show?"

"Sheep and ships. And castles."

Brother Arros and Elena exchanged a glance. She pulled a wad of something from the pouch at her waist.

"Here." She thrust it at the man. "Bark of the willow. Chew it and your pain will ease."

He touched the dry husky mass to his lips and gave it a tentative lick.

"No." Elena bent down and pushed the wad of willow bark into his mouth. "Now chew."

"Do as she tells you," Brother Arros advised. "She is wise in the ways of healing. Far wiser than me or any of the brothers within these walls."

The man lay back, closed his eye, and resolutely began to chew.

Walking back to the guesthouse, Elena stewed over the injured man's words.

"We saw men from the house of Oto on the King's Road two days ago," she said. "Their leader was all in red armor. Must have been the baron or his son."

Brother Arros shook his head. "It was no Oto who struck that man, but their steward. That group stopped here yesterday for ale and bread. They wanted grain for their horses and oxen."

"The baron and his son weren't among them?"

"The steward told me the baron is at Castle Oto. His son Ramón fights the Moors in the south for Queen Isabella."

"What brought them north?"

"He wouldn't share the reason for his journey. He only said that the baron sent him to attend to a matter of trade."

"And he spreads violence along the way," Elena said

sourly. "No doubt he's ordered to do so by his lord. In keeping with the ways of his house."

"Perhaps. Perhaps not."

Elena gave Brother Arros a sidelong glance. "Cruelty runs in that family's blood. It's no secret. Their servants are not spared the whip or the rod. I pity any and all who enter their gates."

"By the sun and stars, I hope I never come across a member of the house of Oto," Xabi said. "Is there not one among them worthy of respect?"

Brother Arros said, "Yes. Lady Marguerite. Ramón's wife."

Elena stared. "You never told me he married!"

"Elena has few enemies, but when she finds one, she drags him behind her on a chain forever." Brother Arros tossed a weary glance at Xabi. "I find it's best to speak of Ramón de Oto as little as possible."

She shot Brother Arros a dark look.

"Lady Marguerite cannot help being married to the man," he pointed out. "It was no choice of hers. She is a good, kind woman. I met her when she was only a child, on her way from Béarn to Castle Oto. I keep up a correspondence with her to this day."

"It's no good to hold *her* up as a respectable member of the family. She's not of their blood," Elena retorted. "She's only a woman, and Béarnaise besides. Has she birthed any boys?"

Brother Arros hesitated, glancing away. "No babies yet."

"If what the gossips and muleteers say about the house of Oto is true, she'd better give them a son before too long."

"That is why I pray for Lady Marguerite each day."

Brother Arros excused himself and hurried out the guesthouse door.

12

SPRING, 1484

Elena walked with Xabi up the steep switchbacks that led out of the monastery's narrow valley to the mountains. The dog followed at a short distance. The spring sun was fierce today, the scarlet and gold of early wildflowers already fading.

It was time for them to separate. Xabi would return to Jaca and hire himself out again to a wealthy sheep rancher. He would join other shepherds and lead the flocks to the high meadows for the summer.

When they weren't tending to injured animals and moving the flocks from meadow to meadow, the shepherds would make cheese, mend equipment, and tool leather. At night they would gather under the stars for singing and storytelling. The men would lodge in tiny stone cottages that had weathered untold winters and provided shelter from summer rainstorms.

"I envy you," Elena admitted. They stopped in the shade of an oak tree and shared a handful of walnuts that she pulled from a pocket.

"What do you envy?"

"Your summertime amusements."

Xabi laughed. "I guess I should've spent more time telling you about the scrapes I've got into with lynx and wolves. The dogs I've lost. The time a bear chased half the flock over a cliff. You'd not be so jealous then, I warrant."

She chewed reflectively, staring at him. "I suppose you'd be bored without such diversions."

He shook his head, smiling. "I'll miss you, Elena."

"And I you." She moved into the circle of his arms and pressed her head against his chest.

Two crows cackled at them from a branch overhead. Elena burrowed into Xabi's warmth, shutting out the sound.

The idea of life without Xabi made her melancholy. The long days of foraging in the hills around San Juan de la Peña had always brought her pleasure—but solitude would feel different now, she was sure. Of course, there were the forays into Ronzal to visit friends, the summer meeting with its feasting and dancing, the joy she took in helping babies into the world, in healing the sick. She brightened, thinking of that. There was much for her to do while the sun shone on these mountains. Even if Xabi was not by her side.

"Next winter, we'll return to your valley together," he said into her hair, as if he knew her thoughts. "It will be just as it was this time. Only better."

Her eyes stung. She closed them, fighting back tears.

He put a hand on her cheek. "You could come with me, you know."

"The other shepherds would want me to cook for them. A woman's nothing but trouble in the high country."

"You're not like other women."

She didn't reply, just gave him a gentle push. "Off you go. Fetch your flock. Winter'll be upon us again before we know it."

"May the gods watch over you until then," he said, kissing her one last time.

"And you."

Elena watched Xabi and the dog climb the narrow, winding trail until they disappeared from view in a dense forest of black pines.

Eyes wet, she started back to the monastery, trying without success to put Xabi out of her mind.

13

SUMMER, 1484

It was the peak of summer. The moon swelled each evening, nearly full now, casting silvery light over the fields and orchards. Elena would leave tomorrow for the high country, to share the revelry and feasting of the mountain people. Her meager belongings were packed, her dagger sharpened. She was ready.

Since Xabi left, she had spent most of her time roaming the hills in search of herbs, roots, and honey. She had harvested more butterwort leaves than ever before, on Brother Arros's request. It was far more than he could use in his infirmary, she'd pointed out, but he muttered vaguely about other plans for the stuff. So she had complied, had filled several ceramic pots with healing ointment and delivered it to him without another word. After all, Elena had never known Brother Arros to be anything but honest and sensible. If he saw a use for her medicines, he could have them. There was nothing she wouldn't do for the man.

The monastery bustled with activity this time of year. The kitchen gardens were bursting with vegetables, the barley flourished under the summer sun in the fields beyond the cliffs, and the flocks had been sheared and herded to high meadows. Meanwhile, the busy industry of wool washing and drying went on without cease. It looked like hot, sticky, backbreaking work, and Elena was glad she had never been asked to participate.

She looked forward to this evening with a thrill of anticipation. Brother Arros had asked her to meet him in the parlor that was normally reserved for high-born visitors. Once, when she was a small child, she had asked to see the room, and now it seemed she was going to get her wish. She smiled. After all these years—Brother Arros had remembered.

"Sit, my dear," he said when she entered the room. He gestured to the chair across from his own.

He held up a letter written on linen paper. A red wax seal dangled from it.

"I have had news from Lady Marguerite," he said.

Elena perched on the edge of the chair, staring at the seal. The wax was emblazoned with two circles of different sizes, overcut by a cross. Brother Arros unfurled the letter so she could see the lines of text.

"Do you forget I cannot read?"

He ignored her impertinence. "The lady asks for aid. She is in a delicate situation and needs a help-mate. I pity her—I have long worried about how she fares in that castle, so far from her homeland, from her family. She has no one."

"She's got servants upon servants," Elena objected. "How can you say she has no one? What about her husband Ramón? What about his parents, the baron and baroness?

You said it yourself: she's part of their family now. Why not ask them for aid?"

"Ramón is away fighting the Moors in the south. Who knows when—or if—he shall return? Her mother-in-law is..." Brother Arros's voice trailed off. His eyes darted away from Elena, a slow flush rising on his round cheeks. He shifted in his chair uncomfortably. She had never seen him look so flustered.

"Her mother-in-law is what?"

He turned his gaze upon her, finding his composure again. "There is little the woman can do for anyone, I fear. And the baron—well, he is best left out of the matter."

Elena crossed her arms over her chest, silent.

"I can only think of one person who can give Lady Marguerite the aid she needs," he said.

"And who's that?"

"You."

The word slammed into Elena like an iron-tipped arrow.

"Me?"

He stared at her steadily. "Yes."

She sprang from her chair and backed toward the door, a wild fluttering in her chest.

"Castle Oto? I'd rather crawl into a bear's cave. You know that as well as I."

"Please, Elena. She is with child."

She put her hand on the door latch, but did not lift it. "So it's happened."

He nodded.

Slowly Elena turned to face him. "And you're determined to do her bidding. To help her."

"Yes. As I once helped you."

"How can you ask me this? Me, of all people?"

"So much time has passed. You are a grown woman now.

No longer subject to the fears of a child. You have brought countless babies into this world, Elena. What is the harm of helping one more?"

"You're ordering me to do this thing?" Her voice shook.

"No. I would never presume to do that. But consider it, please. For my sake, and for hers."

In her head, Elena thought: *Never*.

"You leave in the morning for the mountain meeting," Brother Arros said gently. "Think on it tonight, and bring me your answer before you depart."

Elena's heart pounded crazily against her ribs. She pushed open the door and made her escape.

The next morning at dawn, she left the monastery without giving Brother Arros an answer.

14

The meeting of the council leaders was over, the feast was done. Under an ancient oak in the center of the meadow, the sun-warmed stones that served as chairs for the council rapidly cooled in the evening air. Empty leather sacks of wine lay flattened on a round cross-section of oak nearby. Great golden dogs nosed about in the grass for over-looked crusts of bread and the wizened heels of sausages.

A short distance away, people were gathered around a roaring bonfire. The jangle of a tambourine melded with the insistent beat of a drum. Rhythmic clapping soon broke out. Then a group assembled and began to dance, spurred on by cries of encouragement from onlookers.

Elena and Thérèse de Luz stood a bit apart from the others, watching the revelry in the gathering dusk.

"Each summer I journey to this gathering just to be with you," Elena admitted, slipping an arm around her friend's swollen waist. "I always thank the gods when I find you and Jorge safe and well. This time, I've even more to be thankful for." She glanced down at Thérèse's belly.

Thérèse leaned into her embrace. "I'll need your

wisdom and your kind touch when my baby comes. Can you return to Ronzal with us?"

Elena took one of Thérèse's hands and squeezed it reassuringly. "First I must return to the monastery. Brother Arros has asked something of me, and I owe him an answer."

Thérèse glanced at her. "What is it?"

Elena hesitated. It did not feel right to share Lady Marguerite's news. It was not her place.

"A favor he wishes to promise to some high-born lady. He wants me to be her help-mate."

Thérèse laughed. "Are you sure it was you he asked? Perhaps his sight is going."

"Since I was a girl he's called me a wild thing, worries about me flitting around these mountains getting in scrapes with the beasts that hide in the shadows." Elena sighed. "He's right. I am wild. What good does he think I could do locked inside walls of stone, tending to a lady?"

"He must have a reason," Thérèse said thoughtfully. "He's never asked such a thing of you before."

"True."

"And he's been a friend and protector to you all your life."

"Without his help, I'd be long dead," Elena admitted. "Though the Abbey of Belarac wasn't the sanctuary he'd promised. You and Jorge, the other families of the mountain villages who took me in—you've been my true protectors."

Thérèse turned, an unsettled look on her face. "We'll always share our hearths with you, my friend. But what you say is not entirely true. You've been under Brother Arros's protection all your life. When he sent you to the abbey, it was only the beginning."

Elena stared at her friend in silence, uncomprehending.

At that moment Jorge de Luz approached, arms outstretched to his wife. "Thérèse! Come, you must dance!"

Thérèse shook her head. "I've barely the energy to walk, let alone dance."

Jorge looked at Elena, his warm brown eyes full of good humor. "You, then. You've been dancing around these fires since you were a girl. You've got no baby in your belly, I trust."

No baby. The words barreled into her like a kick in the gut, but she forced a smile. "I'm too busy helping other babies into the world to have one of my own. I wouldn't miss the chance to dance."

He reached for her hand. "I'll deliver her back to you in no time," he promised his wife. "I know you two. Never run out of things to talk about."

The two women did not get another chance to speak until the celebration was over. The mountain people lay rolled in their wool cloaks on the meadow, whispering to each other under the moonlight. Red embers glowed like winking eyes from the smoldering bonfire. The scent of crushed grass mingled with the smoke that drifted through the cool night air.

Elena slid closer to Thérèse, who lay beside her snoring husband. "Tell me what you began to say earlier," she whispered.

Thérèse put her lips to Elena's ear. "After your mother died, the mountain people grieved. Maria was like a mother to many of us, too. She had healed our parents, our brothers, our sisters, our friends. She helped babies into the world, taught their mothers how to care for them. And when Father Pizarro started calling her a witch, when he turned people against her, we tried to make them see they were wrong. But it was no use. My own mother was there at the burning, to witness it. She felt helpless—everyone did. There was nothing they could do to stop it." Thérèse hesitated. "At least the gods took pity on Maria and let her die before she was burned. She got that one small bit of grace."

Elena's mouth went dry. If only that were true. Memories swept over her like bitter gusts of autumn wind, muting the sound of Thérèse's gentle voice.

She remembered with utter clarity the fear that had gripped her as she crept through the woods in the dark to deliver a last terrible gift to her mother. Elena had been spindly-limbed in those days, quiet and cautious, attached like a burr to Maria's side.

During the endless days of Maria's imprisonment, Elena barely ate. She was terrified to be alone in the cottage, consumed with wild fears about her mother's fate. Though she had seen barely ten winters, she knew when word came about the priest's intentions that she would never allow him to carry out his plan.

So despite her terror, she braved the dark woods alone. Heart hammering, she drifted noiselessly through the inky night air to the village church, slipped inside, and made her way to the only person on earth who truly loved her.

When the priest found Maria's corpse behind the iron bars of the holding cell in the church the next morning, he dragged her outside and tied her to a stake before a silent crowd of villagers. Elena stood transfixed among them, suffocated by grief. Somehow she had imagined death would end Maria's suffering.

Stupid girl, she berated herself. Tears stung her eyes.

The thunder of hooves pounded through the woods. The Baron of Oto, his young son Ramón, and their men rode up on sweat-soaked horses, swords clattering, dust rising from the road behind them. The sight filled Elena with hope. Surely the leader of an ancient noble house would put a stop to such madness. The baron would tell the priest to cut Maria down from the stake. He would make order out of chaos.

Still astride his horse, the baron remarked upon the fact that Maria was already dead. But when Father Pizarro asked permission to light the pyre anyway, what did the nobleman do? He pulled off his silver helmet and waved a hand dismissively in the priest's direction.

"Very well," he said in a bored tone. "Light the pyre."

And then he and his men and his son watched Maria burn.

She's already dead, Elena reassured herself as the flames leapt skyward. *Fire can't hurt her. Nothing can hurt her.*

She huddled behind the broad-shouldered blacksmith, averting her gaze. Her eyes were drawn to the men on horseback, to young Ramón de Oto. As he watched her mother's body turn to ash, a luminous smile took hold of his face. It never wavered. He even threw back his head and laughed a few times, his long black hair cascading over his shoulders.

Hatred boiled in Elena at the memory. Perhaps if that had been her only encounter with Ramón, the intensity of her rage might have lessened over the years. But the gods were angry at her in those days, and they devised another punishment. They flung the two children together again not long after Maria's death. That time, there was no blacksmith to hide behind.

Elena had the scars to prove it.

A knot of pine burst in the bonfire, snapping Elena out of her reverie. She forced herself to concentrate on her friend's words.

"After Maria's death," Thérèse was saying, "Brother Arros sent word to Ronzal. He asked us—and all the mountain people who are our friends—to watch out for you, to offer you a place at our hearths, to make sure you were fed and clothed and housed. Though he believed the Abbey of Belarac would be a safe refuge, he understood you well. A wild thing will escape its cage eventually. He knew you'd roam the mountains again, and he wanted our promise that we'd help you. He never dreamed how quickly that day would come."

Elena rolled over on her back, stunned into silence. She had always harbored a tiny kernel of anger toward Brother Arros. After her banishment from Belarac, he had not stepped in. She had traveled the mountain valleys alone, finding comfort and protection from families who remembered Maria. It was Maria's legacy that made her welcome at hearths in every mountain valley.

Or so she had believed.

How foolish she had been.

"All these years," she said slowly, "your kindness to me was done as a favor to him?"

"Of course not." Thérèse felt in the dark for Elena's hand. "You're as much a sister to me as any of the girls my mother birthed. Any kindness we've done, you've repaid many times over. If anything, we owe Brother Arros for bringing you into our lives. Think of the babies you've helped into the world." She placed both their hands on her distended belly. "If it weren't for you, I'd be even more frightened than I already am."

Elena frowned. "That priest—he still lives among the mountain folk, still sometimes interferes with a birth. Has it ever happened in Ronzal?"

"He knows better than to stray too far from the baron," Thérèse said. "He's got no other ally, after all. From time to time we hear talk that he creeps up to the high country to steal the offerings that shepherds leave out for the gods. But more often he sends a village boy to do it for him."

Elena felt a rush of relief. "It's settled, then. Brother Arros awaits my answer. As soon as that's done, I'll come to you in Ronzal."

"And what is your answer for him?" Thérèse asked.

"The one I'm bound to give."

15

SUMMER, 1484

Elena covered the distance from the high country back to San Juan de la Peña with great speed. She jogged steadily through forests of pine and oak, across meadows that shimmered with heat. Her lungs burned and her skin beaded with sweat under the baleful yellow eye of the sun.

From the look of Thérèse's belly, Elena's services would be required in Ronzal before the next full moon. She needed to give Brother Arros her answer, wheel around, and stride back up the mountains again. A pair of crows shadowed her for a while, their black wings whispering through the air. She paid them no heed. There was no time to waste selecting a rock to fling at the shiny beak of a crow.

Finally she arrived at the base of the soaring cliffs where the monastery lay, her hair wet with sweat and her clothes coated with dust. It was mid-afternoon and most of the monks were laboring outside. She caught sight of the familiar figure of Brother Arros in the orchards near the guesthouse. Though her throat was parched and her feet throbbed with pain, Elena rushed to his side and flung herself to her knees.

"Brother Arros, forgive me," she panted, wiping her brow with the back of a hand.

He set down the basket of plums he carried. "What have you done that requires my forgiveness?"

"The kindness of the mountain folk—it was all thanks to you."

She began to cry.

Brother Arros pulled a wine sack from around his neck.

"Here." He handed it over.

Elena drank deeply and took several shaky breaths, gathering her composure.

"I've long known I owe you my life," she finally said. "But I never knew how much you've truly done to protect me."

He held out a hand and pulled her to her feet. "Come now, child. You are a blessing to me. Whatever small comfort I've provided you pales in comparison to the wisdom you share with us. Your ointments and teas have healed more people than you know."

She stared at him through her tears. "Will you never find fault with me?"

He tilted his head to one side, considering her. "No."

"I've come to give you my answer. I'll help Lady Marguerite, though I do not want to."

The relief was clear on his face. "I shall write a letter for you to deliver to the baron. You shall be happy to know he is not there at the moment. A traveler from Zaragoza who lodged in our guesthouse last night told me the baron is in that city, attending to business affairs—to the wool trade in particular."

"Sounds unlike a baron." Elena used her sleeve to pat the sweat off her brow. "Wet swords with the blood of common folk, that's what they do."

Brother Arros rolled his eyes. "I am too busy today to get

embroiled in an argument with you about the habits of noble families."

"Fine. When will Lady Marguerite's baby come?"

"When autumn turns to winter and the days grow short."

"Thérèse de Luz's first child comes sooner than that, and I've vowed to help," Elena said, frowning. "After I go to Ronzal and give her my aid, I'll make my way to Castle Oto."

"I would not dissuade you from helping your friends."

"Mind you, I'll only stay at Castle Oto long enough to see Lady Marguerite's child into this world." Elena's voice rose defiantly. "I'll not become a servant bound to her and trapped within those walls."

"Of course. She does not expect that." Brother Arros patted her arm. "The lady will be grateful for your help. You will pass the time there in peace, and leave again when it suits you."

"You make the place sound all gentleness and light. Do you forget the history of that house?"

Brother Arros sighed. "Would I truly send you into a bear's den? You are a child of God and God will protect you."

"Your God cares nothing for me." Elena put a hand on the dagger at her waist. "I'll protect myself."

After two days of rest, Elena was ready for the journey back to Ronzal.

She waited in the shade by the guesthouse for Brother Arros to finish his morning duties. The atmosphere was charged with energy. Monks streamed around her carrying rolls of flax fabric, jugs of ale, and ceramic containers of grain to a staging area near the stables. Brother Arros flitted among them, dispensing instructions. Finally he came to her.

He held out a small leather sack. "Dried cherries and walnuts for your journey." From a pocket in his robe, he retrieved a parchment scroll fastened with a red wax seal. "For the baron. And his son." His voice grew sober. "They both must read my letter. Tell Lady Marguerite to make it so."

Elena stiffened. "But you said Ramón is at war in the south."

"Even so. When he returns one day, he must know the contents of this letter."

Carefully she placed the scroll in the satchel slung over her shoulders.

"Brother Arros!" called a monk. "Your counsel is needed."

Beyond the stables, Elena saw a column of dust rise across the valley.

"Ah!" Brother Arros exclaimed. "There it is—the mule train at last."

"Who rides with them?"

"Truly, I care not. All I know is they head south, as far south as travelers dare to go, where Queen Isabella's army fights the Moors." He gave her a distracted glance. "The saints above, there is much to do. And before I tend to any of it, I must write another letter and pack more things to send south with those mules."

"I'll be off, then." Elena pressed Brother Arros's hands between her own.

"I shall not forget the favor, and nor shall Lady Marguerite." He glanced around them and drew closer. "There is something else you must know before you leave. A secret you cannot share with anyone, not even Xabi, nor Thérèse. Do I have your promise?"

Elena nodded.

"Quickly, now." He bent his head to hers, whispering in her ear.

When he finished, she turned away in silence.

Following the steep path to the clifftops, she mulled over his words. Help-mate indeed. Accomplice was more like it. Unwilling participant in a reckless plan that would likely end in tragedy. But still, she had made her promise. And a small part of her felt vindicated. The barons of Oto were every bit as cruel as she believed.

Her breath grew quick and shallow, her heart shuddered in her chest. Come autumn, she would find a death cap in the woods and tuck it in her satchel. For as much as she pretended otherwise, mustering the courage to enter Castle Oto would require more than a dagger and a quiver of arrows. A noble house presented far greater dangers to a mountain woman like her than any beast of the wilderness.

And whatever happened, she vowed grimly, her life would not end within those walls.

16

SUMMER, 1484

The village of Ronzal had long been Elena's refuge, but this night it seemed an entirely foreign place. Wolves haunted the outskirts of the village and men took turns patrolling the hillside with torches and resin-tipped arrows, dogs at their heels. Everyone else was shuttered inside their homes. The unnatural silence outside was interrupted only by the occasional howl of a wolf. Heat had scorched the mountains for days, and the air inside the cottage was thick and still.

Elena coaxed Thérèse to stay upright, telling her stories, wiping her brow with a rag soaked in lavender water, giving her sips of wine. She had learned long ago from Maria that a first labor went better for mother and baby if the pregnant woman kept moving. After hours of pacing and squatting, of leaning on the backs of chairs and on the stone walls of the cottage, exhaustion finally forced Thérèse into bed.

While Thérèse rested between labor pains, Elena went to the door and peered out the small square that was cut into it at eye level. Dusk was creeping over the mountains, cooling the earth. The shimmering moon had begun its ascent into the purple sky. She imagined an invisible thread attached to its round face, pulling it slowly upward.

A memory struck her of a birth that had occurred on a night such as this, still and hot and illuminated by a full moon, not long after Father Pizarro arrived in the mountains.

The night everything went wrong.

Maria had pulled her outside the Guerrer family's cottage during a lull in the long labor. They gazed overhead, watching the moon begin its silent climb.

"Look," Maria said, pointing at a long band of stars that stained the night sky with a pale haze. "The pilgrims in Brother Arros's infirmary say those stars light the way to Compostela. Some of them die on the trail there, following those stars."

"Why do they go, then?" asked Elena, squinting upward. The stars did seem to be aligned in formation.

"It's to do with God," replied Maria.

"Are we going to do it?" asked Elena. She hoped not.

Maria laughed. "No, girl. We're not like them."

"But I've seen you praying!"

"I pray to the gods of the mountains—gods we'd best not anger. I pray to keep us safe from their rage."

"What do you mean?"

"Blizzards, floods, wind storms. Those things happen because people make the gods angry."

Elena tried to imagine what an angry god looked like. A giant red face contorted with rage floated into her mind. "I hope I never make them angry."

Maria hugged her close. "Don't worry, little one. Children are innocent. The gods only get angry when people do evil things."

"Like what?"

The exhausted woman on the bed let out a long, wavering moan.

Distracted, Maria turned away, her reply smothered under the sound.

But Elena did hear one word of her mother's answer: *Murder.*

She had never heard the word before, so she had no reason to fear it. And yet, watching her mother return to the pregnant woman's side, Elena's chest tightened with a spasm of dread. She fought the urge to rush forward and bury her face in Maria's skirts.

Balling her small fists, she prayed to the gods for the first time.

There was only one thing she asked of them: to bring Ulricca Guerrer's baby into the world safely so that she and Maria could go home.

Ulricca Guerrer had been married for many years and had been pregnant at least six times. And yet the Guerrers still had no children. Several of the pregnancies ended in miscarriage, and the two babies that Ulricca gave birth to were stillborn. This time the pregnancy seemed normal enough, but the labor went on too long. Ulricca lay flat on the bed, sweaty hair plastered to her face. Her eyes were closed.

"Dip a cloth in that cool water and bring it to me," Maria murmured to Elena.

Maria wiped the damp cloth over Ulricca's face, smoothing the tangled hair away from her forehead.

"Why does it not come?" Ulricca croaked. "Why?" She grimaced, overcome by a wave of pain.

"It will come," Maria said confidently. She took Ulricca's hands in hers and squeezed. "Push again. Find the strength."

Veins bulged on Ulricca's neck as she bore down. A deep groan burst from her chest.

"I see the baby's head!" Maria cried.

Elena crouched next to the bed, watching the baby's dark head bulge outward. The skin around the crowning skull was stretching, stretching, stretching. Elena knew sometimes it split open, spilling blood everywhere. But Maria rubbed ointment on it, waiting, giving the skin time to stretch.

"Now, Ulricca," Maria said after a few moments. "One more big push."

The woman took another deep breath and bore down again. The baby's entire head emerged, and with unusual speed, the rest of its body followed. Maria stared at it in silence, and Elena rocked back on her heels.

The baby, a boy, had only one wizened arm. That was why he slipped out so fast. His tiny legs were twisted, as if the bones curled within them. Yet he lived. He opened his round mouth and let out a tremulous mewl.

Ulricca lay back, spent. Tears mixed with the sweat on her face. "I want to hold my baby," she whispered.

Quickly Maria wiped the baby clean and wrapped him in a linen cloth. "Go call for Señor Guerrer," she whispered to Elena. "Hurry."

When Señor Guerrer strode up to the cottage, there was another man at his side. A priest. As he approached Elena, the polished wooden cross he wore around his neck caught the moonlight, glistening.

The two men entered the cottage. Elena hung back just outside the door, watching them advance on the women. Her entire body thrummed with fear.

"I've a child!" Señor Guerrer boomed. "Is it a boy or a girl? Father Pizarro, you must lay your hands on our baby, give it your blessing."

Maria put a restraining hand on his arm. "Wait!" she said sharply. "I must talk to you first. There's something wrong with the child, his limbs—"

"Wrong?" the priest interrupted. "What do you mean? Let us see for ourselves."

He strode to the bed and examined the swaddled baby. "There's nothing wrong with it."

Maria unwrapped the baby. At the sight of his deformed body, Ulricca began to cry. Her husband let out a shout, then covered his mouth with his hands and sank to his knees.

Father Pizarro crossed himself. "This is the work of the devil!" he said. "It is meant to curse us. Cover it up again!" He held up his cross as if to ward off evil emanating from the tiny body.

Ulricca turned her head away from the baby and sobbed. Her husband stared wild-eyed at his newborn son.

The priest pointed at Maria. "*You* had something to do with this dragon child."

Maria shook her head, backing away.

"Señor Guerrer said you are always here to attend the births." The priest took a step toward her, one hand cupped protectively around his cross. "And yet never have their babies survived. Now the gift of a child at last—but instead this poor couple must endure the birth of a monster. I suspected as much. You have cursed this family."

Maria scrambled away, skirting around the two men. The priest reached for her arm, but she slipped past him and made for the door. Señor Guerrer leapt forward, stuck out a foot and tripped her. Maria fell face-first onto the beaten earth floor.

Elena's heart pounded in terror. How could these men treat her beloved Maria so viciously? She took a wobbly step forward. The priest put a foot on Maria's back, pressing her to the ground.

"Your days of freedom are over, witch." He held his cross aloft.

Elena froze, her eyes on the cross.

"You have slithered through these mountains spreading evil for far too long," he hissed.

Maria ignored the priest. Lifting her head from the ground, she looked frantically for Elena. There was an expression on her face that Elena had never seen before.

"Run, girl," she cried.

The words hurtled through the air and thudded against Elena's ears. She would not do it. She would not abandon her beloved mother to these hateful men. Resolutely she took one more step forward.

"Run!" Maria said again, in the ominous, flat tone that was reserved for moments of danger. She had trained Elena early on to obey that voice without question. And now, like a puppet on a string, Elena did as she was ordered.

She wheeled around and fled into the night.

Thérèse cried out, wracked by a labor pain. Elena hastened to her friend's side, angry with herself. Why had she dredged up the sorrows of the past again? Her nightmares would return. Dark worries would seep into in her mind, chipping away at the hope she had reclaimed during her winter with Xabi.

She bent over Thérèse, whispering encouraging words. It was time. The baby was ready to emerge. Elena helped Thérèse onto her side.

"Grip my hand and push now," she said.

Thérèse bore down with all her strength, unleashing a mighty groan. The baby's head began to crown.

"If it's a boy," Thérèse said hoarsely, her bloodshot eyes on Elena, "We'll call him Arnaud."

"And if it's a girl?"

"She'll be Elena, after you."

17

AUTUMN, 1484

A fter a fortnight of tending to Thérèse and her new son, Elena left Ronzal on a cool, drizzly morning, headed to a cave that lay a day's journey to the east. These limestone mountains were porous, full of gaps and holes and secret spaces. People had long used caves as refuges from the gods, from the beasts of the wilderness, from the swords and arrows of enemies. And Elena held a map in her head that showed the location of each one.

As her journey through the mountains progressed, the air grew crisper each day, the beech leaves in the forest turning from green to gold. Thérèse and Jorge had gifted her a new cloak of hand-spun merino wool before she left, dyed black with boiled walnut shells, and she was grateful for its warmth and softness.

On the third morning, she left her limestone refuge in a light rain. Dark clouds pressed down upon the ridgetops and she wrapped her cloak tightly around her to ward off the chill of dawn.

Before long she reached the grove of black pines where Maria had taught her to harvest death caps. She found the ancient tree in their midst, the one that bled pitch and bore the marks of passing bears, its trunk riddled with holes drilled by woodpeckers. Pulling her dagger from its sheath, she quickly harvested the largest death cap she could find. Upon a moment's reflection, she collected one more.

Rolling the scarlet-topped mushrooms in a length of flax cloth, she tucked them at the bottom of her satchel. When last she stood among these trees she was a girl not ten winters old—a tormented little thing, driven by fear to creep into the darkest woods in search of poison.

She stood motionless, listening to a woodpecker drill a hole in the trunk of a nearby pine. Maria had taught her how much could be learned by studying trees. Which way the wind blew, what kinds of animals made their homes nearby, if there was water flowing unseen below the roots. How Elena missed those precious days spent in her shadow.

Maria always told her she was a gift of the mountains, the best gift she'd ever received. And Maria had received many gifts in her lifetime. She helped untold numbers of babies into the world, healed countless injuries and illnesses. The mountain people loved her. In return for her services, they gave her wool, sausages, tools, stacks of dry oak kindling, precious packets of sea salt, kegs full of wine. No sooner did a crack open in her roof than it was fixed.

But all that changed when Father Pizarro arrived and began peddling his one great God, muttering about something called the Devil, hissing to all who would listen that Maria was no healer but a witch.

Witch.

How Elena hated that word. Father Pizarro had unleashed it on the most vulnerable people—those whose loved ones had died despite Maria's help. He whispered to the grieving that Maria was to blame for their losses. And some of them, in their agony, believed him.

The woodpecker fell silent. Elena turned slowly on her heels, willing herself to move east. The rain was heavy now. Her journey was nearly over. She had just two more stops to make before she entered Castle Oto.

It did not take long to reach the stone cottage where she had spent her early years. The structure stood on a south-facing meadow in the shadow of an oak tree. The tree's drooping branches disguised the true condition of the place until she was nearly upon it.

Elena stood on the threshold, gazing around at the wreckage of the home she had shared with Maria. There was no longer a door. Rain poured through the roof. Gaping holes scarred the walls. It looked as if people had been salvaging bits of the place and carrying them away. A squirrel darted out from a shadowy corner and clambered over the rubble into the woods. An abandoned bird's nest lay on the dirt floor, fragments of cream-colored eggshells scattered around it.

There was no point indulging in memories here. Dry-eyed, she continued on her way.

When she reached the outskirts of the village where Maria had died, a low rumble of thunder swept down from the white peaks in the north. Raindrops struck Elena's face like needles in the fierce wind. She pulled the hood of her cloak low over her forehead and stood under cover of the woods, watching the storm descend.

Sensibly, the villagers were nowhere to be seen. The cottages were dark, their doors latched and windows shuttered. The church was shuttered, too, though its wide oak door rattled in the wind, creaking and banging as if the latch were loose. The rope affixed to the church bell whipped around like a writhing snake. Elena stood in the shadow of a pine tree, watching the action of the rope and the wind conspire to swing the bell back and forth. Soon the sound of faint, discordant chimes drifted over the village.

Her mind darted back to the night she had entered that church for the first and only time. The night of Maria's death. What she had done must have angered the gods, but they had not seen fit to punish her. Not yet.

Suddenly the church door opened and the priest emerged to fiddle with the latch. He closed the door experimentally. The rattling continued. He opened it again. His body had softened, his shoulders sloped under his black robes. He was an old man now. Yet still he lived.

Elena's hand went to the dagger at her waist. She took a step forward.

How easy it would be to exact her revenge. She could slip behind the church, sidle along the edge of it to the stairs, and strike. She slid the dagger from its sheath and took another step.

Who would see her? The storm boiled in the sky, the villagers were ensconced in their cottages. She would deal her death blow swiftly. Though the priest had not planned a merciful death for Maria, she would show mercy in delivering his. For Elena had no interest in torture. All she wanted was to extinguish him, watch his blood drain out and the light in his eyes ebb away. And then, perhaps, the pain of her memories would be extinguished as well.

At that moment, a braying mule cantered around the back of the church, its hooves clattering on the cobblestones in the square. The frayed end of a rope dangled from its bridle. Clearly it had been spooked by the storm and somehow tugged free of its bonds.

Elena's pounding heart slowed.

The moment of opportunity was gone. No villager would let a mule run loose, no matter how dangerous the storm. Sure enough, a man wearing a tattered flax shirt and a pair of wool leggings burst from his cottage and made for the mule.

The priest caught sight of the man and called out to him. The villager ignored the priest and tended to his mule, calming the animal. Waving his arms and shouting, the priest moved down the church steps with his robes flapping in the wind. This time the villager shouted something in return, gesturing to his mule and then to the church. The priest seemed satisfied with the man's response and retreated inside.

Elena knew Father Pizarro had never found his way into the hearts of the people. They tolerated him because they had no choice. They sat through his sermons, they carved wooden statues of the Virgin Mary and slung them around their mules' necks, and still they prayed to the old gods.

He was nothing like Brother Arros, whose kindness and compassion made him a favorite of guests at the monastery, whose essential goodness radiated from him like the rays of the sun. No, Father Pizarro was a different sort of religious man, whose contempt for the old ways would always make him an outsider, someone not to be trusted.

She sank to her knees, the bitter wind searing her face.

Somehow, in the space of a day, she had become a hollow, scooped-out shell. The smiling woman who had lain beside Xabi all winter in a snug stone cabin was gone, floating away in a current of swirling air, as weightless as a ghost.

All that was left of her was bone and skin, pressing east through the sodden forest, moving farther and farther away from everything that was good in this world.

Her mouth set in a grim line, Elena sheathed her blade and forced herself to stand.

It was time to fulfill her promise.

18

AUTUMN, 1484

Afternoon was giving way to evening. The clouds parted to reveal the setting sun, its light lengthening the shadows in the woods. But then clouds pressed low again, bringing with them frosty gusts of wind and sleet.

Elena was close to Castle Oto now. She strode along animal tracks that paralleled the main trail, as was her habit. It was never wise to travel in the open. She would rather meet her end in a bear's jaws than under a bandit's blade.

She approached a clearing and a ramshackle cluster of dwellings inhabited by serfs who were bound to the house of Oto. They were desperately poor, the serfs, somehow scratching a living from the earth with meager harvests of barley, carrots, and turnips. Those who lived near the great houses of Aragón were fated to be miserable, for they never escaped their lord's attention.

And the house of Oto had always been brutal to its serfs. The women were never free of harassment. Often the more attractive daughters of these families were sent to the castle, ostensibly as servants, fated to be concubines for the baron and his men.

The wind died away. It was replaced by an eerie quiet. Usually at dusk the jays and crows kept up a constant racket, and snow finches could be counted on to trill warning calls at a person's approach. And yet the birds had gone silent in these woods.

Elena slowed her pace, uneasy, and caught sight of a movement overhead.

A great bird winged its way down from the sky into the clearing. It looked very much like a griffon vulture. Why would such a bird alight in a barley field? Elena crept forward to the edge of the woods.

The field had been scythed, the grain harvested—quite recently by the looks of the place. Ragged stubble rose from the dark earth. And in the center of the field, not one but three griffon vultures feasted on a carcass.

Elena's eyes narrowed. No wonder the blue jays and crows had gone mute; they'd been frightened off by the giant raptors. The griffon vultures clustered together, tearing at their prey with great stabs of their powerful beaks. What was it they had there? A deer, perhaps? The serfs were not skilled hunters. Even if they had managed to kill a deer, they would never leave the carcass to scavengers.

She moved through the woods along the edge of the field, nearing the cluster of rude huts where the serfs lived. Then she saw three horses bearing Oto livery tethered to a tree nearby. Gruff voices shouted from within one of the huts, followed by a high-pitched scream. A sick feeling took hold of Elena's stomach.

With sudden certainty, she knew the carcass in the field was no deer.

Elena's hand went to her dagger. Clutching the handle,

she wrestled with the urge to act, to help those pitiful souls inside the cottage who were likely being beaten or raped at this very moment.

But what could she do? Three horses meant three armed men. She would become their victim, too, as soon as she made her presence known. The parchment letter in her satchel would mean nothing to them. She would be dispatched as easily as a rabbit if she tried to defend these people.

No, if she wanted to live, if she wanted to someday return to her winter valley and find comfort in Xabi's arms, she would have to ignore the savagery before her.

Elena turned away and melted into the woods again, desperate to escape before another shriek pierced the air. But she slipped and skidded on the wet leaves, her trembling body unable to do as her mind commanded. Finally she forced herself to stop, steadying herself against the smooth, cool trunk of a beech, waiting until her breath returned to normal.

She removed the sheath from her waist and strapped it around her thigh. The cold handle of the dagger pressing against her flesh was reassuring.

Then she squared her shoulders and set off once more, fanning the flames of hatred that always glowed within her heart. She ruminated on the rage she felt for that priest, for the barons of Oto, for all armed men who abused their power. And soon her strides came quicker, the fear loosened its grip, and a surge of confidence coursed through her veins.

Thank the gods, she thought.

For without courage, she was doomed.

19

AUTUMN, 1484

Elena stood at the edge of the forest, looking out at icy drizzle that was rapidly turning into snow. Castle Oto loomed above her on the hilltop. Beyond it, serrated peaks thrust upward like knife blades into the darkening sky. Her throat was dry, though she'd just drunk water from the stream that rushed through this copse of oaks. Dread had sucked every drop of moisture from her mouth.

In the gathering twilight, she emerged from the woods and trudged up the grassy hill. The Oto banner fluttered from stone towers that soared above her, impossibly tall. Torches burned atop the high walls surrounding the castle, sending long tongues of fire into the air. A guard on the parapet caught sight of Elena moving through the grass and shouted to a comrade below. When she arrived at the gates, a helmeted head peered out from the window cut into the center of one of the massive wooden doors.

"What's your business here?" the guard asked gruffly.

"My name is Elena and I've a letter for the baron from Brother Johan Arros of San Juan de la Peña."

"A letter, eh?" The man stared her up and down. "Show me your face," he ordered.

Elena stiffened, but did his bidding and pushed the hood of her cloak away from her forehead. "I am to be help-mate to Lady Marguerite," she said. "The lady expects me."

"Is that so?" He eyed her a moment longer and slammed the window shut.

The heavy door swung open.

"In you come, then," he said.

She forced herself to cross the threshold. The guard reached out a meaty hand as she passed and tugged at the bow strung over her shoulder. He took hold of her quiver and gave it a rough shake.

"You're well-armed for a woman. But you'll have to leave your weapons here."

"They're for hunting," she protested. "And protecting myself from the beasts of the forest."

He shrugged. "I don't make the rules."

Reluctantly, Elena handed over her bow and quiver.

"What else have you got?" He stepped closer. Elena smelled ale and onions on his breath. "What's in that satchel?"

"Medicines and other things for the lady. The monks have my promise to deliver them to her unmolested."

He snorted. "Unmolested? Wouldn't want to disappoint the monks, I suppose. Well, on your way then. Hurry along. It's nearly supper-time in the castle. If you're lucky, they'll feed you before they feed the hounds."

Walking up the winding lane toward the keep, past the tiny cottages that housed castle dwellers who weren't lucky enough to have noble blood, Elena comforted herself with the thought that some of them were of mountain stock themselves. Some had family she had tended to in the hills and valleys beyond these walls. Perhaps she would even see a familiar face.

But darkness was descending, a wet snow was falling, and no one was about. The cottages were already shuttered against the night. Muted voices emanated from inside their walls.

As she crossed a wide courtyard and approached the doors to the great hall of the castle, a deep, hollow bark made her flinch. Soon another hound joined in, then another. From the sound of it, they were big hounds. She dragged her boots forward, though every muscle in her body screamed at her to turn and run.

Elena climbed the broad stone steps to the doors. An iron knocker in the shape of a bear's head was affixed to the oak just above eye level. She stared at it for a long moment, the courage she had mustered in the woods leaking out of her with each breath she took.

Slowly, slowly, she reached for the knocker, her arm heavy as stone.

Then she let her arm drop and whirled. She would not do it. Promises be damned. This was madness.

And then there was the sound of an iron bolt being flung back, the creak of the door opening behind her.

Gulping for breath, trembling, she turned around again.

20

AUTUMN, 1484

The guard on the other side of the door dispatched a servant girl to lead Elena to Lady Marguerite's chambers. Elena edged past the drooling hounds, trying to steady her breath, desperate to gather the shreds of her courage again. She kept her head down, following the girl through a maze of corridors and stairways that had no discernible logic. Torches mounted on the walls barely cast enough light to see more than a few steps ahead. After a final climb up a twisting set of stairs, they arrived at a tall door fitted with decorative iron hardware and a protruding lock.

Inside, despite the flames shimmering in a cavernous fireplace, the air was cold. Red woolen rugs worked with Moorish designs were spread over the floor. A four-poster bed hung with heavy drapes stood against one wall, and a low oak chest squatted against the wall opposite. An iron candelabra fitted with eight beeswax candles sat on a round table that held a collection of carved wooden boxes. The windows along the exterior wall were fitted with wooden shutters that trembled from the force of the wind.

Lady Marguerite was seated in a leather-backed

armchair before the hearth, wrapped in furs and woolen blankets. She turned her head, told the servant girl to wait outside. Then she trained her gaze on Elena.

"Come, approach."

Elena walked forward a few paces.

"So you are the help-mate Brother Arros has sent to me." Lady Marguerite spoke in a low voice. Her pale green eyes with their long black lashes were unnerving.

Elena nodded.

"Did he tell you the nature of my predicament?"

"Yes."

"If God answers my prayers, your job will be easily done. But if He does not—?"

The words took a long time to slip from Elena's throat. "I will carry out the plan as Brother Arros asked me to do. I've promised him that."

"Good. Perhaps, if God is merciful, nothing shall have to be done."

"Perhaps."

"You must speak of this to no one." Lady Marguerite leaned forward and lowered her voice to a whisper. "The castle is like a beehive. All the bees fly about gathering gossip, for it is honey to them."

"And who is their queen?"

Lady Marguerite gave a short laugh. "There is no queen. All the honey goes to the steward. And, when he is home, the baron."

"What about your husband?"

"Ramón is never here long enough to bother with gossip," Lady Marguerite said shortly.

Wind rattled the shutters and sent a draft into the room, snuffing out two of the candles on the table. Elena jumped at the sound, her eyes darting to the windows.

"The north wind sweeps down from the mountains without end," Lady Marguerite said. "Come winter, there is no respite from the noise of it, nor the cold."

"You've a fine hearth and a crackling fire. Furs and woolens to wrap yourself in. I suppose that helps." It was difficult for Elena to scrape the sneer from her voice, but she managed.

Lady Marguerite stared at her coolly, then threw back the furs and blankets and heaved herself up from the chair.

Elena stared back. The woman was fine-boned and much younger than she had expected. Dark coppery hair peeked out from under the hem of her silk head-covering. Her dress was red, made of some thick fabric that had a dull sheen, and the sleeves of her blouse were criss-crossed with tiny black stitches laid out in an elaborate pattern. How her tiny frame supported the enormous belly bulging under her skirts was anyone's guess.

"Do you feel sick?" Elena asked abruptly.

"Yes. I must force myself to eat."

"You don't force quite enough down your gullet for my liking. You're much too skinny."

Lady Marguerite advanced toward Elena, eyes narrowed, scrutinizing her with a hard gaze. "*My lady*, you mean to say. Brother Arros sings your praises. I wonder if you treat him with such rudeness. Somehow I doubt it very much. I shall not tolerate such behavior, even from a low-born mountain woman like yourself."

"Yes, my lady." *So there's a bit of spark in her after all*, Elena thought.

"You'll stay in a cottage outside the keep," Lady Marguerite said. "When I have need of you, I'll send for you as it suits me."

"And what am I to do otherwise, my lady?"

Lady Marguerite looked surprised. "I know not."

"I tend to the sick at the monastery and in the mountain villages. I could do that here. Heal wounds, nurse the ill."

"Ah?" There was a glimmer of interest on Lady Marguerite's face. "Perhaps we could use your skills."

"I'll have to come and go, glean what I need from the woods and the fields," Elena went on, feeling emboldened. "For ointments and the like."

Anything to escape these walls, she thought.

"I do not see the harm in it," Lady Marguerite said after a moment. "Perhaps you can help the baroness. She suffers so."

"What ails her?"

Lady Marguerite's expression tightened again. Her eyes slid away from Elena's.

"I'll do what I can to help her, my lady," Elena said when it became obvious that Lady Marguerite was not going to answer. "There's an herb in the woods around here that cures all manner of ills. But I shall have need of my bow and arrows if I'm to go out harvesting," she added. "The gate guard took them from me."

"I shall see they are returned to you."

Rummaging in her satchel, Elena pulled out the parchment letter. "Brother Arros asked me to get your promise that both the baron and his son will read this."

Lady Marguerite looked surprised. She reached for the letter.

"I shall see the baron gets this as soon as he returns from Zaragoza," she said.

"Who watches over this place when he is gone?" Elena asked.

Lady Marguerite gave her a sharp look. "The steward, of course."

"But the steward also goes abroad, my lady."

"How do you know that?"

"I saw your steward on the King's Road near the pass to Béarn in the spring." The sight of him in his red leather armor astride the great black horse still haunted Elena's dreams. "Brother Arros told me he visited San Juan de la Peña with his men."

Lady Marguerite frowned. "The men of this house travel widely, and I am privy to their plans only as it pleases them. But I do know this: when the baron is away, the steward cannot stray far. He goes out for the day, hunting with the guards, or punishing those who would cheat my father-in-law of the goods they owe him."

Elena's mind flashed to the serfs, to the griffon vultures feasting on the body in the field. Had the steward's horse been one of those three tied to the tree outside the huts? She recreated the scene in her head. Yes. Two of the horses were dun-colored, and one—the largest horse—was black.

Her gaze dropped to the roll of parchment in Lady Marguerite's hand. She did not like the idea of that letter falling into the steward's grasp.

Lady Marguerite saw the worry in her eyes.

"Fear not." Crossing to the oak chest, the noblewoman opened it with a key strung on a golden chain around her waist, then laid the scroll inside. "When the baron returns, this letter will be delivered into his hands. And when my husband comes home from war, it will await him in the Tower of Blood. That I promise you."

Elena's throat went dry again. "The Tower of Blood?"

"It is on the south side of the castle. My husband's chambers are there." Lady Marguerite locked the chest and straightened up. "Violence always visits this place from the south, you see. Violence and sorrow."

There was something new in Lady Marguerite's voice. Was it anger? Elena couldn't tell. The woman was a stranger, after all. It would take time to discern her character, sort out her moods.

"A girl awaits you in the corridor," Lady Marguerite said, her voice clipped and formal now. "She will take you to the kitchens for supper, then to your cottage."

Lady Marguerite stared at Elena expectantly.

A moment passed. Then another.

"Oh," Elena said, realizing what Lady Marguerite was waiting for. She executed an awkward bow. "As you wish, my lady."

As Elena and her guide descended the stairs to the great hall, she saw to her relief that the dogs were gone. Her eyes roamed around, taking in the sight of heavy wooden chests and tables laden with gleaming silver-plate. The walls were hung with tapestries. She counted six bear skins on the stone floor. An earthy, musty stench filled the air, a scent of rotting hides and mold mixed with the acrid smell of smoke from the torches that blazed on the walls. In the very center of the hall hung a circular chandelier made of deer horns. It looked like a thorny crown ablaze with fire. Elena stopped underneath it, mesmerized.

"How do the flames stay alight?"

"It's got an iron frame inside," the servant girl said. "That's where the candles are stuck."

Glancing at the girl's face for the first time, Elena saw a purple bruise on her cheek. The skin on her neck was riddled with long, scabbed-over scratches.

"What happened to you?" Elena asked.

The girl's expression hardened. "I'm the steward's favorite."

"That's what he does to his favorite?" Elena reached out a hand to touch the girl's cheek, but she flinched and stepped back.

"Soon enough he'll tire of me, or put a baby in my belly."

The girl could not have been more than fifteen. Yet her eyes were sapped of life, her shoulders hunched like an old woman's. The energy and hope of youth had been chased out of her long ago, by the looks of it.

"Listen," Elena said, leaning close. "I've got remedies for what ails you. Seek me out and I'll help you. Even if he does put a baby in your belly—I can stop it from coming."

"Why would I want to stop it? He'll leave me alone if my belly swells, turn his sights on someone else." The girl smirked. "Maybe you."

At that moment, a group of women swept through the doorway of an adjacent room, wearing dresses with long, trailing sleeves, their hair covered with lustrous fabric. In their midst was a lady dressed even more richly than Lady Marguerite, with a pearl-studded cap on her head and a cloak of russet-colored fur over her shoulders.

The servant girl dropped into a deep curtsy.

Elena stood staring as the group approached. She had never seen such finery. One of the women locked eyes with her, frowning. With a swift movement, she reached out and slapped Elena across the face.

"You offend the baroness!" she hissed. "Bow down, you insolent creature."

Elena's cheek stung. She crouched, fighting the urge to slap the woman back. Under her lashes she watched the baroness totter past. The noblewoman did look ill. There was an odd glaze to her eyes, and she stared aimlessly at the skirts of the woman in front of her, completely disinterested in her surroundings. A gold belt around her waist was strung with a medallion. It bore the same design as the wax seal on Lady Marguerite's letter to Brother Arros.

The baroness was talking to herself, Elena realized. Murmuring something under her breath. Her whispery voice was high, like a child's. The sound of it unsettled Elena nearly as much as the sight of the griffon vultures feasting on the carcass in the field. She watched the wobbly progress of the baroness over the bearskins, transfixed.

A drop of hot wax oozed off a burning candle in the chandelier overhead then, splashing on Elena's hand. She quickly flicked the wax away, blowing on her skin to cool it. When she looked up again, the entourage of women had gone.

"Let's be off," the servant girl said. "You won't last long here, will you?" There was a note of sympathy in her voice now that had been absent before. "From now on, you see a fine-dressed person, you bend the knee."

Elena did not respond.

"What, you've never bowed to your betters? You highborn yourself, then?" The girl folded her arms, her eyes glittering with malice. "Where's your fancy dress, your jewels? Why is your hair a tangled rat's nest, and not piled high on your head?"

"Just show me the kitchens," Elena said wearily. "Please."

Elena followed the girl down another staircase into the bowels of the castle. A roar grew in her ears as they approached the cavernous kitchens—the rattle of copper against iron, the chatter of coarse voices, the clank of ceramic cups and bowls. The servant girl walked into the melee without a backward glance and Elena hesitated in the doorway a moment, paralyzed by an unaccustomed shyness. But no one even looked her way when she finally slunk into view, so immersed were they in the business of filling all the bellies in a noble house.

Seated near the hearth at a rough table with a bowl of steaming soup before her, she shrank into her cloak, wishing she could follow smoke up the vast chimney and vanish into the black sky. She wished she could shut her eyes and open them again to find that all of this had been a nightmare. She wished for the wings of a bird so she could leap out the windows of Lady Marguerite's chamber and fly away.

But none of those things would happen.

Elena was part of this now, part of castle life.

And it was every bit as mad a place as she imagined.

THE END

Elena's story continues in *The Girl from Oto*. Turn the page to dive into a free sample...

AMY MARONEY

THE

GIRL

FROM

Oto

How far would you go
to unveil a secret kept for 500 years?

PROLOGUE

Summer, 2015
Pyrenees Mountains, France
Zari

Silver threads of rain twisted down from the dark sky. A chaotic wind swirled around Zari, shifting and billowing from all directions, tugging at her backpack with invisible fingers. She stabbed at the slick trail with her trekking poles. It took all her concentration to stay upright.

At the edge of a broad meadow, she watched massive gray storm clouds curl in on themselves, gather speed, silently collide. A blaze of light ignited the sky above the mountains. Counting the seconds until the rumble of thunder began, she eyed a nearby pine forest. The lightning was still miles away. If it got close, she would take cover in the sheltering edge where the trees met the meadow.

A spike of adrenaline took hold of her. She was no mere observer. She was part of this great spectacle, a bit player in a dazzling show of power. Wading through the tall grasses, she let their waterlogged heads tickle her palms. A dark trail in her wake charted her progress. She would mark off the entire meadow this way, stride by stride, searching for a story written in stone.

On her third traverse of the meadow, she stumbled and fell. Heaving herself up, she untangled a kink in the chain around her neck and tucked the shell that hung from it back in place at the base of her throat. Another flash of lightning. For an instant, the sky turned a bleached bone-white. The boom of thunder that followed reverberated in Zari's chest long enough to scare her.

She had not taken five more steps when she saw them.

Rows of half-sunken stone slabs jutted out before her like shards from a giant's pottery collection. Sinking slowly into the earth, corroded by wind and rain and ice, they offered themselves up to her. Foundation stones. Evidence.

"I knew it was here!" she shouted, waving her poles in the air.

She turned in a slow circle, imagining the buildings that once spread across this land, protected by a high stone wall, by the sharp spires of iron gates. She saw a church with a soaring bell tower, a bustling kitchen, a garden filled with vegetables and herbs. In the murmuring wind, she heard the voices of long-dead women and children.

Then a dark shape materialized across the meadow. A tall figure moved toward her through the grass. A man. She stood mesmerized, vaguely aware of the crackling sky, the growl of thunder. She could almost see waves of sound rippling through the heavy wet air.

He walked quickly, cutting through the raindrops with long decisive strides, narrowing the gap between them.

Zari swallowed.

She took one step backward and tightened her grip on the poles.

BOOK I

Ab initio. From the beginning.

1

Autumn, 1484
Castle Oto, Aragón
Elena

Like the breath of an angry god, the wind streamed over the mountains from the north and slammed into the castle. The balcony shutters bucked and heaved, straining against the iron latches that held them in place. To Elena's ears, the sound was the hollow clacking of bones. Wind goes where it wants, she thought, finding the source of a draft with her fingertips. She closed her eyes and imagined herself in the forest, where brittle leaves swirled in unruly flocks and golden-eyed owls blinked in the high branches of oaks.

A faint moan rose from across the room. Elena straightened up, squared her shoulders. The sooner they got on with it, the sooner she could escape these walls. She rolled up a small woolen rug and wedged it against the base of the shutters, muffling the rattle. Then she padded across the thick Moorish rugs to the great bed and pulled aside the drapes.

The young woman lay curled on her side. In the candle-light, it was difficult to pick out details, but Elena had dressed and undressed this body so many times that she did not need the aid of the sun to understand the predicament. The woman—still a girl, really—was built like a snow finch. Her belly was far too large for her bony frame. For months, Elena had traced its bulbous arc with her fingertips, measuring the swell of it, prodding the taut skin. The likely explanation was not a giant, but twins, and for a first birth that often meant catastrophe.

She dipped a cloth into a copper pot of water that sat on the floor by the bed. With practiced movements she bathed the woman's pale limbs, smoothed back her tangled hair, massaged lavender oil into her skin.

"My lady, the baby can't wait any longer."

Silence.

She raised her voice. "Lady Marguerite! There's more yet to do. Rouse yourself!"

"Why do you shout at me so? Will you not let me sleep?" Marguerite turned her head toward Elena, her eyelids half open.

Elena felt uneasy, looking into those eyes. They were silvery green, like the hide of a tree frog, and the black lashes that framed them were spindly as spiders' legs. Perhaps it was this contrast of light and dark that made them so unsettling. Or the long, slanting sweep of them. Or their size, for they seemed much too large for the woman's angular face. Whatever it was, there was something more feline than human about them, and Elena had never been fond of cats. She looked away and put a hand on the distended belly.

"If you wish your baby to die, by all means sleep." Something hard—a knee? A foot?—pressed against her palm with urgent, fluttery movements. "If you wish your baby to live, then push. Now make your choice."

The glowing eyes found hers. A pale slender hand slipped into her strong brown one. The young woman on the bed took a deep breath, set her jaw, and bore down.

The night was half gone when the baby was born. She squirmed and flailed her limbs, gulping air into her lungs and pumping it out again with wild shrieks. Elena cleaned her, swaddled her, and thrust her into her mother's arms.

Marguerite bent her head over the baby. "A girl. God help me."

The newborn quieted and stared unblinking at her mother. After a few moments of utter stillness, she opened her tiny red mouth and began rooting for a breast.

"She will be called Miramonde," Marguerite said softly. "One who sees the world."

"How much can a girl see from behind a wall?" Elena asked.

Marguerite shook her head. "She will not be caged. When she is old enough, she will learn the ways of the mountain people."

Elena stared. "Who will teach her?"

"You."

Words of protest rose up in Elena's throat. But before she could speak Marguerite convulsed in pain again.

"Ah—I thought as much," Elena said, careful to keep a neutral voice. "Twins."

"No," Marguerite moaned. "That cannot be. What if it is another girl?"

"Then we'll be doubly grateful to have a plan in place."

When the second baby slid out of his mother's womb, Elena held him aloft so Marguerite could see what she had birthed. He was a tiny, red, crumpled thing, smaller than his sister. Elena rubbed him briskly with a piece of clean linen and blew on his drowsing eyelids until he opened his mouth and emitted a faint wail.

"An heir. My husband will be pleased."

Marguerite's voice was low and rough, but whether that was due to emotion or exhaustion, Elena could not tell.

"If he survives the war," Elena said.

"Talk like that can get you whipped. Have a care."

"Who is going to hear? Your father-in-law is bedded down with his favorite wench, and the steward's lame back has made a thief of him."

"What do you mean?" Marguerite's bloodshot eyes flickered to the door and back.

"Poppy milk. He's got your mother-in-law's bedtime habit now. Head lolling on the cushions, drooling. 'Tis not a pretty sight."

Another gust of wind barreled down from the high peaks, and the shutters struggled against the rolled-up rug. Thump. Thump. Thump. Elena hurled an irritated look in the direction of the balcony and got back to the business of cleaning and swaddling the boy. She tucked him under his mother's arm and led his pursed red lips to her other breast. For a time, they listened to the babies nursing and the soft thumping of the shutters.

"In the space of a moment, you have slandered my husband's parents and their steward. I have seen serfs lose their heads for less damning words," Marguerite said finally. "I placed all my trust in Brother Arros, bringing you here. I wonder now why he places his trust in you."

Elena shrugged. "I'm a creature of the mountains. Never learned to talk like a lady."

"You can start by biting your tongue. There are no secrets in this place."

"Tell me, my lady, if there are no secrets in the house of Oto, why am I here? We'll fail before we even begin."

"I order you to cease your prattling and your impertinence grows."

"I've simply asked a question, my lady," Elena shot back. "A fair one."

"Our plan will succeed. It must. And now you'll do your part to keep her safe."

A tense silence settled over them until the baby girl fell asleep. Elena plucked her out of her mother's grasp and wrapped her in a length of soft wool.

"When all is said and done, you've two healthy babies," she said. "And one of them a son. The luck of that."

Marguerite closed her eyes, one hand on the necklace at her throat. "Yes. The luck."

There was a stable boy Elena trusted, whose mother she had healed from illness on two occasions. She drew her cloak shut to conceal the sleeping baby swaddled against her chest. Bending over the boy's nest in the straw, she gently woke him and asked him to fetch a certain horse that she knew to be steady and calm. He readied the mare and helped Elena into the saddle. She squeezed his hand in the dark.

The horse clopped down the stone alley to the castle gates. The guards were not surprised to see her; she often came and went at odd hours.

"Good evening, my lady!" called one. "Look at you on that fine horse."

"I'm not one to put on airs, you know that well enough," she said in as light a voice as she could muster. "Even poor mountain folk like me are given a favor now and then."

The men unlatched the heavy iron crossbars and the great oak doors swung open.

"Are you not afraid of wolves and bears?" the other guard asked.

"Those creatures fear the moonlight. Puts them under a spell, it does."

He snorted. "The beasts outside these gates fear nothing but fire and iron."

Elena forced out a laugh and prodded the horse forward. Behind her, the crossbars clanged shut. She turned her head and spat. An urge rose up in her to yank the horse's nose due west and gallop hard all the way to Basque country, to the edge of the world where the rivers flowed into the sea. Instead, she dug her heels into the horse's belly, guiding it deep into the mountains.

For there was no point wasting her thoughts on idle fantasies.

She would not betray a promise.

❄

THE MIRAMONDE SERIES

The Miramonde Series tells the story of a Renaissance-era female artist and the modern-day scholar on her trail.

The Promise is a prequel novella to the series. *The Girl from Oto* is Book 1; *Mira's Way* is Book 2; and *A Place in the World* is Book 3.

To learn more or to buy books in the series at your favorite online retailer, please visit www.amymaroney.com.

For a free six-chapter sample of *The Girl from Oto*, go to BookHip.com/RGNFRV.

If you enjoyed this book, please consider leaving a review at your favorite online retailer—or spread the word with family and friends.

ABOUT THE AUTHOR

Amy Maroney lives in the Pacific Northwest with her family. She studied English literature at Boston University and public policy at Portland State University, and spent many years as a writer and editor of nonfiction. When she's not diving down research rabbit holes, she enjoys reading, hiking, drawing, dancing, and gardening.

Connect with Amy:
www.amymaroney.com

facebook.com/amymaroneyauthor

twitter.com/wilaroney

instagram.com/amymaroneywrites